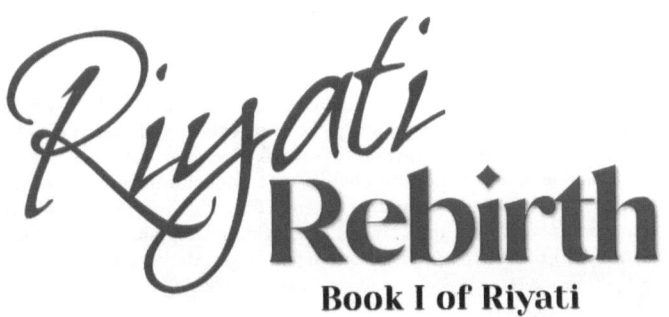

# Riyati Rebirth

## Book I of Riyati

Kai Zeal

aquakat
publishing

Aquakat Publishing

Published by Aquakat Publishing
PO Box 656
Pinson, AL 35126
aquakatpublishing.com

First edition: August 2024
Second edition: February 2025

First Edition Cover Design by Emory Glass
Second Edition Cover Design by Kai Zeal
Second Edition Cover Glyph Illustration by amagren

ISBN 979-8-9923922-0-3 (eBook)
ISBN 979-8-9923922-1-0 (Paperback)
ISBN 979-8-9923922-2-7 (Hardcover)

Human Creativity Badge by Conrad Altmann

# content warnings

The viewpoints and actions in this book do not necessarily express the viewpoints of the author. **The following are depicted, described, or implied within this book:**

*Alcoholism, blood, child abuse, classism, death, decapitation, emotional abuse, extreme violence, gore, homelessness, hostage situations, kidnapping, murder, needles, loss of a loved one, parental neglect, physical abuse, poverty, sex trafficking, stalking, strong adult language, substance abuse, suicide, and torture.*

**Reader discretion is advised.**

To the marginalized and abused,
to the forgotten and neglected:
May the night bring solace and the dawn bring hope.

# table of contents

# Chapter One

## shattered glass

"Did you hear? It happened again," a girl beside me said to her friend, hushed whispers. "Another person went missing. No trace of their body. Cops can't find anything."

I pulled my phone out, scrolling through my social media feed. Everyone kept talking about this — probably was just people running away; it wasn't like there was much else to talk about in this city. Usually, we imported our drama fresh from Savannah, but people started going "missing" over a month ago, right as we came back from holiday break. And it's all I'd heard about since then, from Dani, from my classmates.

It didn't affect me. I wasn't stupid enough to roam outside at random hours, go down dark alleyways with strangers following me. I'd never even been to detention, though knew more about it than I probably should thanks to Jordan being a frequent visitor. Speaking of, I picked my duffel bag up as I saw him walk out the front doors of the school, searching for me in the spot I normally stood.

"Sorry, you wait long?" he asked as he rubbed the back of his neck.

I shook my head. "Not really. You ready to go?" Speaking of reasons I was long past ready to leave, I heard a couple behind

1

me giggle as they whispered, "What's she see in him anyways?" I just rolled my eyes; it was Friday, and I was ready to spend the night watching movies with Dani, not listen to the high school rumor mill — which had been the same as the middle school rumor mill and the elementary rumor mill before that. Jordan and I'd always been friends. Just friends. I had my plate full enough just trying to keep Mom happy — she was determined I'd go full scholarship to a major university, and I was on my way there; wasn't really sure what to do once I got there, but that was a problem I didn't have to deal with right now.

His ice-blue eyes lowered to grass as he nodded, walking a step or two behind me as we left our high school. I was spending the night with my oldest friend, Dani, as we usually did on Fridays, had for as long as I could remember, switching between houses. We usually met at our local park and walked together to whoever's house we were staying in that night. Jordan's house was around the park, but despite knowing him for just about as long as Dani, I still wasn't exactly sure where. Apparently was nearby though, so he usually walked with me to the park before heading home.

Stretching, I took in the pleasant March breeze — most of the year sucked here weather wise; summer was always humid and hot, and winter was still humid, which made the cold more biting. Really, a lot of my problems were with the humidity, thinking about it. "I'm not looking forward to that geometry test next week," I said.

"Dunno how you do that shit to begin with," Jordan said.

"Because Mom said so." Often, I envied his life, where he didn't have parents breathing down his neck about every grade. I'd only ever made one D on a quiz, and that was back in middle school. It'd earned me a three-hour lecture, being grounded for a month, and Mom *helping* me with my homework for weeks afterward. I'd gotten a lecture about how some universities wanted to pull back to middle school grades for admissions. Even now, it felt overboard, but as long as she was happy, she left me alone to actually enjoy life.

Also, I hated math, but I hated art class more. Stupid thing never made any sense — I wanted a *solution* to copy, not pretend I actually cared about the assignment.

The faded wood sign reading "Opal Pines Park" with amber lettering finally came into view. I didn't see Dani at the entrance — she was taller than Jordan or me and had auburn hair, so it was pretty easy to see her at a distance usually. Guess we got here first, which wasn't that surprising — our high school was closer to the park than hers, but she usually got out of her final period before I did. Seems they kept her the full time today.

Glancing around, I saw a few people from school walking around. There was this little girl, couldn't have been older than six, bright red hair and dark green eyes, a sundress on. Seemed cold for this weather, but she looked scared more than cold. Her eyes kept darting between people, as if one would take her at any moment. Where were her parents?

"Oh, she's here," Jordan said, his voice soft. I saw Dani approaching us out of the corner of my eye, but I couldn't look away from this little girl. I felt bad, how scared she seemed.

"Tell Dani I'll be back in a minute. Just want to check on that little girl." I didn't wait for his answer as I walked over to the child, kneeling as I approached her. "Hey, where's your parents?"

She sniffled as she pointed further back, closer to the forest section of the park. The only thing our city was really known for was the forest — lots of pine trees, to the surprise of like no one. Was a protected forest or something, where no one really went in there.

"What's going on?" That was Dani; she and Jordan were behind me, her hand on my shoulder. "You know the brat?"

I shook my head. "You want us to walk you to your parents?" The little girl nodded, taking my right hand and pulling forward. I followed where she took me. If nothing else, it seemed to give her the courage to go wherever her parents were. Closer and closer to the forest edge, she led me — well, us, since Jordan and Dani were behind me still, Dani closer as Jordan trailed behind us all. As I saw the park path began circling back around to the front, I paused. "You see them?"

She let go of my hand, running into the trees; disappearing from sight, I heard a childish whimper. Had she fallen? I followed her, searching around. But I saw nothing but trees

3

that might as well have blocked out the sun, like it was night out instead of late afternoon.

Dani moved closer; I felt her warm arm move against my torso as she stepped in front of me. "Something's wrong." Jordan had caught up; he hadn't said anything, but he was right beside me, behind where Dani stood. I struggled to maintain my balance against the leaves and branches in between the grass as Dani pushed me backward. This yellow blur collided with her, with where I had been, and I heard her scream like I'd never heard from her before. Shrill, chilling, not a sound that should've come from a girl I'd always considered invincible: she had a black belt, could kick and punch and... whatever else people with black belts did. Dani screamed again before she lost consciousness. It was some type of large cat, had gripped Dani by the arm, teeth sinking into her flesh before throwing her against the tree like some rag-doll.

All too suddenly, I understood: this was what happened to all those missing people, wasn't it? It wasn't a dark alleyway in the middle of the night, wasn't people running away.

Jordan bumped into me while stepping backwards, away from the child.

It was my fault. I just wanted to help.

The little girl pet the enormous cat — tiger? Lion? Leopard? I couldn't think clearly enough to pretend to figure it out. It purred, licking Dani's blood from its claw. "Good kitty," she said.

Dani was unconscious, but at least I saw her still breathing. Blood still trickled from her arm, not to mention whatever shots she'd need from a wild cat bite: she needed to get to a hospital. I wanted to flee, get away, survival instincts crowding my mind at the realization if others hadn't made it out, we weren't likely to either. I couldn't leave Dani behind, leave Jordan behind; he stood still, hands trembling.

I didn't know what to do. Didn't know how to respond, how to —

A "hmph" came from the little girl as her head gestured toward Jordan and me. That large, ashen-furred cat strode closer — where had this thing even come from? It didn't look like any of the large cats I'd seen advertised in the Savannah Zoo, didn't even have stripes, only a smooth single colored coat.

Its steps were even, controlled. How did this little girl even domesticate it? Who — what — was this little girl to have that type of power over a cat that looked to weigh more than she did?

Only a yard out, it suddenly dashed toward Jordan and myself; all I could do was close my eyes and brace for pain, expecting worse than I'd ever experienced judging by Dani's screams.

I felt no pain though, only liquid dripping onto my bare arm: Jordan gasped, a ragged wince soon after. Eye shooting open at the sound, I saw Jordan's arm in the cat's mouth, a sickening crunch soon after as he screamed. The cat drug him out by the arm, shaking him around like a chew toy, hind legs ripping through Jordan's jeans and into skin. Each scream dug into my soul, my legs and arms growing heavier, begging for movement, but it was like invisible weights were attached.

I did this. Caused this. Dani had blacked out. Jordan was far worse: would've been better off unconscious, not him screaming in ways I hadn't even heard in the few horror films I'd snuck over the years.

The large cat kept yanking, like it was trying to separate Jordan's shoulder from his body, his knees from his legs; its claws dug further and further in, fur covered in matted red from Jordan's blood.

He didn't even scream as the cat picked him up by the shoulder and threw him into a tree, body sliding down into the overgrown green grass now stained red. The iron smell made me want to vomit, but I was still too scared, too petrified to move, like some small animal that hoped to hide by being silent and still. Except I had no doubt she knew I was there. How Jordan was alive yet alone conscious, I genuinely didn't know. He had strained breaths as a soft sob slipped from his throat. Fresh blood dripped everywhere, through his mauled jeans, his olive-brown hair matted with deep red, blood across his face like a rusted tattoo that could never be erased. I saw muscles like a health class info-graph, but it wasn't some far off lecture, said tendons exposed to the naked eye.

Something was wrong. Something familiar. Like a glass plane shattering in my mind and why. Why was it familiar? I had never seen something like this before, not even in a movie theater, not in the most attempting-to-terrify-me-into-being-healthy health class video.

"We're going to eat well the next few days, aren't we, Kitty? There's some mana with this one especially." The girl stroked the cat's blood-smeared fur, no care of the sticky blood now on her fingers. It began purring once more, nuzzling her.

There was nothing I could do. I was next and I wasn't even sure how much I cared: Dani needed immediate medical attention, and Jordan made Dani look perfectly healthy and peppy with how much worse he was. He was still conscious, and I wished he wasn't. I wished I wasn't conscious either: at least Dani wasn't awake for the end.

He whimpered; I took a step back, my mind somehow simulating the pain he was in, my limbs stinging and burning despite nothing happening to me. Well, happening *yet*. Was rather obvious what was coming next, just the question of if it would be quick like had been with Dani or would be worse than the worst I'd ever experienced as had been with Jordan.

*"It's your choice,"* a feminine voice said; there was no one around, but it was so clear, so distinct, like she was right beside me. *"Death is easier, make no mistake. Is that what you want though?"* I shook my head, the smell of iron overwhelming me further. Every strained breath of Jordan's echoing through my chest. I didn't know where the other woman was. I didn't see anyone new, but I couldn't take my eyes off the large cat. It felt like blinking would mean instant death. *"Then repeat after me: Riyati, establish connection, initiate verification."*

What choice was there? The words flowed almost naturally from my lips, softly spoken because I could barely speak at all: "Riyati, establish connection, initiate verification."

"What was that?" the little girl asked.

Another strained breath, gasp, vision I couldn't see but felt throughout my being. Everything was a fog, confusing and disorienting and *painful*.

The voice continued: *"Access stored blueprint, bind to aura for direct withdrawal and simulation."*

"Access stored blueprint, bind to aura for direct withdrawal and simulation." Light shot out from under my feet, runes and characters I couldn't identify raised from the surrounding grass.

Where was the light coming from? What were these runes, each outlined in either an aquamarine or grayish blue color like a continuous gradient, centering around me.

The little girl's eyes, which were an electric green, widened in excitement. "You're one of us? Why didn't you say so — "

*"Phrase set: Riyati, obey your mistress's command, activate withdrawal."* The voice didn't care about cutting the little girl off, and quite frankly, if this other woman had a plan, it was better than anything I could pretend to do at the moment.

But... what *was* I even saying? This voice, this woman I couldn't see but sounded like myself yet wasn't me at all but was so close to me somehow — was I losing it? The lights shone brighter, the humidity even denser than usual for our springs, gusts of sudden wind blowing my hair in all directions. Yet I continued repeating after her voice. What other choice did I have? We were all dead either way. "Phrase set: Riyati, obey your mistress's command, activate withdrawal."

"But how?" the little girl murmured to herself as she stepped back, her confidence shattered.

*"One more time: Riyati, obey your mistress's command, activate withdrawal."*

"Riyati." There was a pull from deep within me, the wind increasing to an almost tornado centered on those strange characters that surrounded me. Thin streams of water circled around me. My lungs burned. I didn't know why. Didn't know anything. "Obey your mistress's command, activate withdrawal."

The runes disappeared, wind and water that I hadn't even realized were supporting my entire body mid-air vanished. Black spots overran my vision before my mind died out.

At least I had tried.

# Chapter Two

# who are you

Jordan | March 24
Opal Pines Forest

Water splashed along my face. Or I thought it's water, could've been more blood for all I knew. The freak wind vanished as quickly as it'd come. Now there's silence, leaving us as we'd been b'fore: waiting to die by being mauled by a goddamn oversized house cat. I had no fight, couldn't scream for Kylie to run. To not be subjected to the blinding pain shooting through my shoulder and legs and fuck, just *everything*? Trying to muster any strength I had, I opened my eyes — everything's blurry as fuck. Smeared outlines. Yellow blob, which had to be the damn possessed feline hellspawn. Thin red blob near it must've been that demonic shit. So much green from the grass and brown everywhere, nauseating amounts of red closest to me. But where's Kylie?

Another voice, one that definitely ain't Kylie or that little shit or Dani, spoke; it's so close to Kylie's but was more mature, confident. "Never a dull day."

"Who *are* you? That magipoten — how'd... that's impossible to increase like that, not that fast..." The shit's voice had a squeak that hadn't been there b'fore.

I clenched my eyes shut, trying to open them afterward. No

**9**

good, did shit-all to help me see anything important like who'd put fear into our demonic hellspawn attacker. My every breath's a strain, worse than any hit I'd ever dealt with. Didn't dare try to move my left arm, if I even could.

"Good question," this unfamiliar woman said. "But not one you're getting an answer to. Would be a waste of time considering you're about to die."

The yellow blob smeared away from me and toward the new woman. Blue was all around her, a stark contrast to the reds and yellows and greens of the other smeared colors I made out between the black spots I saw damn near everywhere.

She didn't scream, unlike Dani, unlike me; the overgrown house cat's the one that let out a loud wail, dropping to what must've been grass since the yellow blob was suddenly surrounded by green. How'd a single woman tame that damn thing? That damn cat threw me around like its bitch.

The thin red outline moved closer, cold hands against my neck. A sting at my throat, something cold and metallic against skin; I swallowed and felt the sting deepen. "I'll kill him if you take a step."

"Pretty sure you won't actually."

The red-haired shit winced. Her hands dropped from my neck to graze my shoulder, and then off me completely. Something heavy dropped onto my jeans, cold from the brief contact it made with my skin. Everything felt cold, sweat intermixing with blood across my body. I'd puke if I could, but I couldn't get the strength to see, let alone puke. "You..."

"You know, your greed started my hell. I don't think there's enough of a thank you I could give. But we must try, now don't we?" A second passed before the woman sighed. "Maybe no fun actually. It's your lucky day." I heard a loud thud beside me, no response from that shit killing us all like it's some game. More liquid seeped against me, but this time, it felt thicker than the freak hurricane, sticky, and *everywhere*, red and brown blurring together and erasing any green I could make out. Lumpy textures pressed into me, almost...skin colors. But from where? Who?

Kylie?

That blue color came closer; who'd saved me, and what'd she plan on doing to me now that the shit was quiet? I felt warmth, calm and comforting, as fingertips brushed against my cheek. "Steady," the strange woman said, her voice suddenly soft, almost gentle. A turquoise and gray-blue color engulfed her momentarily as her fingers held my cheek, warmth from her skin yet a cool leather texture from her lower hand.

This brief flash of pain shot through me, but it just as quickly steadied back out and then... disappeared. A light throb to my head, vision coming into focus. The fuck?

She's close to me, her left partially gloved hand against my cheek, kneeled to where I was slumped against the tree. Didn't seem to even notice the blood all around, dried and wet and still flowing, despite it getting on her otherwise clean clothes, particularly the back section of her coat or dress or whatever the hell it was where the fabric was longer, probably to her ankles normally, the soles of her black boots now deep scarlet. Blood'ed even gotten in the tips of her waist-length braided hair, but it couldn't've been mine —

Holy goddamn fuck.

My eyes widened: it ain't just me here, not just me and Dani and Kylie, dozens of mutilated corpses in various states of decay all around me, including under me I realized as I felt the throw up actually make it to my mouth this time; I turned and barfed, seeing more rotten corpses, flies around them and various states of decomposition and more shit I wished I'd never seen. My heart raced as I felt hands on my shoulders, a firm yet surprisingly gentle push that forced me back into sitting against the rough tree bark. There're no corpses directly where I sat. Who *was* this woman?

"W-who...?" I tried to ask, my throat dry. Resting against the tree, I took in that there're bodies everywhere, including the red-haired shit that almost murdered us all. Unlike the mauled and decaying bodies around me, she looked almost alive outside of her head being ripped from her neck, like a clean slice separating the two, blood dripping from each side. Another body in the pile. Just like I was supposed to be, like Dani had nearly become, like —

Where's Kylie? What'd that bitch do to her?

"Was an illusion to draw people in. Disappeared when she died, but it was impressive to maintain during a fight, will give

**11**

her that." The woman who'd saved me stood, turning from me. Her long reddish-brown hair swayed with her movement, blood caked from her calves down. It's like she didn't even register that though as her eyes glanced, searching for something. I tried to follow her gaze but couldn't make anything out until she walked away and returned with another red-head: Dani, unconscious, bleeding, but compared to myself and the surrounding corpses, not actually looking like complete shit. She sat Dani down on the tree next to me as she kneeled to Dani's unconscious form. The same color of the coat-dress thing she wore, that aquamarine and clouded-blue that had shone so brightly when I could barely see, shined around her left hand as she touched Dani's neck. The blood flow from Dani's head almost immediately stopped. Dani seemed fine if not still out cold. But...

Where's Kylie?

The woman moved Dani onto her back, arms supporting Dani by holding her from behind. She turned to leave, a panic shooting through me at our savior leaving b'fore I knew what'd happened to Kylie. Gripping the bark, it stabbed into my palm as I shakily pulled myself to my feet. How the fuck was I just "shaky" though? Staring at my right palm, I flexed my fingers. No pain, only a mild stiffness. The ever-loving fuck's going on?

I swallowed, eyes searching, a numbness at seeing the surrounding bodies. There's just one I had to find, had to know. "Kylie?" I called. Where was she? None of the bodies looked like hers, 'specially around the area she'd been standing.

The woman half turned b'fore her head lowered, not completely facing me. "She's okay." She re-secured her grip on Dani and then turned around to face me once more. I wasn't sure how she held Dani in the first place, given Dani's taller than myself and this woman's actually shorter than me, closer to Kylie's height. "She's probably going to be out for a little while. She's okay though. Safe. She'll be at school on Monday, I promise."

She didn't give me a chance to argue why her promise should mean a damn to me, instead somehow disappearing right b'fore my eyes with Dani.

I didn't know what the fuck just happened or how to even

process what I'd seen. But what choice did I have but to trust her given that she'd saved us from a certain death, even if I understood none of what'd happened.

# Chapter Three

## siani riyati

"Who are you?" It had been years since I heard that voice, and it was honestly hilarious how much anger could swell up from an objectively valid and harmless question. Being confronted with five years of internalized anger all at once really led to a dilemma of how to react.

Blackness all around: a subconscious principality. My younger self's subconscious principality, to be precise, where not just my younger self, but also those *before* me, her, us, resided. It'd been a while since I had been in one of these, a physical manifestation of the mind, a home for the soul. Everyone had one, but to say only a few knew about their existence was an understatement.

"That's a complicated question," I said. Felt weird to address myself fully as Sia, but it was finally time to truly claim that name for myself. "If you're looking for a name, Siani. Siani Riyati." My younger self was still very unconscious, unsurprising for the initial cycle. Her absence was especially ironic given that she was the technical host between the others I saw and myself, yet she was completely void of representation. Including myself, four women currently had an active presence.

First was a woman around my age, light blue-green eyes that were harsh, judgmental, demanding, long reddish-brown hair in a high ponytail: Kisate Riyati. Near her was a younger woman, bright light blue-green eyes and shoulder-length reddish-brown hair, a nervous fidget with her fingers as she curiously glanced toward me: Chloé. Away from the three of us was the final participant in the current conversation, a woman in her late teen's, reddish-brown hair reaching near to her elbows, light blue-green eyes watching like a cat stalking a mouse, ready to pounce but taking its sweet time to do so: Leah.

...Okay, maybe the cat metaphor was going a bit far given I'd had an unfortunate run in with one hours prior. Must've still been on my brain a bit more than I realized.

"There is no *Siani Riyati*," Kisate — the original question asker — stated, matter of fact, no room for debate. Unfortunately, I didn't take well to other's orders.

"Hm. News to me then because that would just open up even more questions, wouldn't it?" I could feel hostility and distrust and impatience radiating off Kisate. Arrogance. Kisate thought this was her game, her show, as it had been in the past. That time was over; the dead didn't get center stage, that was a privilege of the living. Leah was just as distrustful of me as she kept, kept her distance away from us, arms across her chest as she leaned against an invisible wall. That was one perk of a subcons: walls and floors and pretty literally everything was just mental manifestations, all real yet completely within a mental realm. Therefore, if a person within the subcon wanted and believed there would be a wall behind them, it'd happen. Chloé was still glancing between Kisate and me, lips opening then closing, not willing to say anything while Kisate was in *this* kind of mood.

To be fair to Kisate and Leah's distrust, Kisate was technically correct in that "Siani" shouldn't exist, was a name with no owner. However, their understanding was flawed because the correct answer was there wasn't a Siani *yet*, and if I wasn't here, there almost certainly would never be one. After all, that was one of the primary reasons I was within my younger self right then: to assure my past became my younger self's future. I saved my younger self, Jordan, and Dani. Healed

Jordan and Dani, sneaking away to Dani's house as expected, creating an absorption device for my younger self to permanently wear from this point forward. Once I released the transformation that created the illusion of my body and access to more mana than my younger self would have until my age, her body unsurprisingly collapsed into the pullout bed she had slept in numerous times prior. Her mental capacity had checked out way before that point even, not making it but minutes past her Act in the forest.

But since Act *had* occurred, the wall enclosing the previous three incarnations away from contact with the current crumbled. That was how I arrived at my current situation of being a rather unwanted guest. It was fine: I was their key. Their weapon. All I could be at this point in my life, after all.

"I'm asking once again: *who are you?*" Kisate repeated.

Mock half bowing, I maintained eye contact. "Siani Riyati, as I said, *Your Highness.*"

Right as Kisate was about to argue further, Leah cut her off. "Assumin' that's true, why're you in this subcon? How'd you take control of the body? There's no fifth cycle yet. Nor really anyone who knows Riyati exists, let alone enough to claim its name."

I leaned her hand onto my hip, placing my weight there. "Correct. But there's five people within this one body regardless." Leah wasn't the only one who played games.

"You weren't here this whole time. Your existence didn't suddenly populate until her — " Kisate said.

Fine, I would oblige them with actual answers; anything to take satisfaction away from Kisate. "My birth name is Kylie. Kylie Morgan Rae." I ran my eyes across the other three women, their bodies outlined in the blackness, as if natural lighting was upon each yet nothing else being remotely around. "Fourth incarnation to Kaku Kiseti Kisate Riyati, next in line for Koneku of Riyati when it existed two-thousand years back."

"You're not her. We've watched Kylie, and she's..." Chloé said, one hand holding the other in front of her body. Childish and innocent and insecure; when she died hundreds of years ago, she was younger than me. I felt that naivety, the willingness to trust and believe me at face value. Was something I envied, truthfully.

"I'm not *your* Kylie. She's unconscious, which I'd be surprised if you weren't all aware of already."

Leah's eyes slit, gaze intensifying as she focused on me. Was trying to get a read on me no doubt, look for a weakness or exploit, something to figure out how to direct the conversation. Best of luck to her; my enemies had searched for the same thing and all of them were now underground. Well. Not *literally* right then, but would be in the years to come. Time was both relative and difficult to express when from the future. Also, many of them hadn't actually had bodies to bury by the time I was done, but that was a whole other tangent I really wanted to go off on but couldn't because Leah cut my thought train off with more questions. "Again, say we believe you. How're there two of 'you' then?"

I brought my finger to my lips. They could figure it out if they wanted, but I wasn't telling my exact methods. I liked my cards as close to my chest as I could get them; no one to screw them up that way. "I'm her from the future, I guess you'd say. I'm twenty years old." As Leah opened her mouth, I shook my head. "You can believe me or not, doesn't really matter. But my role is to assure *I* get to continue existing, so I'd say we're all in agreement on the fundamental priority of keeping 'Kylie' alive. And fact of the matter is, you, Kisate." I turned my gaze to the eldest incarnation. "Have absolutely no practical combat experience. And Leah, you know hand to hand, but your specialty is all stealth. And Chloé's never seen a battlefield in her life." I licked my lower lip. "I believe I've already *demonstrated* I know what I'm doing. And if anyone would like to challenge me, by all means. Benefit about being dead is you can't actually *die* and all, so I won't have to worry about holding back."

Kisate glanced at Leah, who shrugged. I had won; what could they do, kick me out? They didn't know how I was there to begin with. Of course, Kisate was the one who spoke, more arrogance in her self-directed role of *the authority figure* emanating from her. This was going to be a long ordeal with this headache around. "So you know what's coming? And that she — *you*, if your words are to be believed — are on a timer now."

"I'm here, aren't I? Actual flesh and bones, I'm sure you can all tell." Taking in a breath, I felt my younger self stir — must've already been the next morning; no way was she up before then, but it was so hard to tell time in a subcon, no windows or lights or clocks. "Don't mention him. That's the only request I have. In exchange, she will live, that I swear."

"Wait, but why?" Chloé asked. "She's already — "

"Of course she has. But this is something she needs to learn herself. See for her own eyes. Come to her own terms with, assuming it's even possible."

# *Chapter Four*

## hectic

Kylie | April 22
Rae Residence

That Friday almost a month prior had changed everything, and I felt it no more obviously than right that second: Sia and Kisate were arguing about how to ruin my Saturday morning, imposing *training* every Saturday since they had entered my life. Meanwhile, Dani had already sent three text messages this morning, angry that I had been too busy for our usual weekend hangouts. I would've preferred watching movies and listening to her talk about her school drama and listening and all those other far more mundane things, but I hadn't been given the choice, borderline locked in my bedroom for *magic training* from demonic supposed *other incarnations* and even my own supposed *future self*.

Contrasting Dani's irritation was Jordan, who had been quietly supportive, if not cautious. I really could've used a lot more of that in my life at the moment from near everyone involved at this point. Less than a month ago, prepping for the SAT was my biggest concern. But Sia insisted some invisible *danger* was incoming, so I was yet again locked in my bedroom, staring at the blank sheet of notebook paper on my desk. The only reason I even entertained her vague, far away monster under the bed was the fact that she was here at all. Something happened that day that should've never happened. I was never alone now, at most one or two of them *sleeping* periodically. Why disembodied voices needed *sleep*, I wasn't sure, but each of them definitely slept, even often during similar times as myself, as I had found out the few times I needed to use the bathroom during the middle of the night. Their sleep didn't completely overlap mine though, with Leah always up incredibly late and rarely woke up before eleven; Kisate was up before my alarm went off every morning and mentally shut herself away rather early in the evening. Chloe took frequent afternoon naps, making me rather envious during class. Sia was the weird one, often up later than myself and half the time awake before me. Always alert, like waiting for some monster to jump out from under my bed while we slept.

*"Any knowledge in foundation needs to start with the written system,"* Kisate's tone was harsh, matter of fact.

I took a deep breath: here they went again. Sia wanted to teach something about theory or "magic" or something; I hadn't been paying enough attention to even know the context of the argument and that had been the correct call given Kisate's tone; they'd be at it for the next half hour easily. I *felt* vague annoyance, like an itch in the back of my mind, something that had been ongoing since that day when I felt Jordan's injuries like my own. *Empathy*, as Sia had called it, was apparently a skill or sense or something of mine now, where I felt the emotions of others around me.

Half unconscious, I fiddled with the ring chained onto a necklace around my neck, something already around my neck when I had woken up the morning after everything. It was supposedly important, something I always had to wear. Who knew if that was right or not, though there was an internal warmth to the ring... at least to me. When Dani touched it, cuts rapidly formed across her fingers where she'd made direct contact. She had wanted an explanation for her sudden injuries, and even now I didn't really understand why she was hurt and I was comforted. I would fidget with the ring often when bored during these studies and no one was around but otherwise kept it hidden under my shirt so no one else was hurt like Dani had been.

The doorbell rang, leading to an exhale of relief from my lungs: pretending to be "normal" took precedence over everything else; I needed no excuse to close the notebook where I had been waiting to take notes since Mom was out at some work function. Afterward, I opened my bedroom door and walked down the white wooden steps to the ground floor so I could open the front door; most of the town home was on the ground floor with only my bedroom, bathroom, and a closet with stashed holiday decorations on the second story.

Like a sudden noise or flash or other mildly painful sensation, I felt emotions flood my head, raising my heart rate with... was it annoyance? From who, Kisate? Shaking my head, that wasn't it. Kisate's emotions felt different, but I couldn't figure out how. She *was* annoyed, but this was from something else, something not from within me. The doorbell rang again, leading to me opening the door.

Oh. That explained the annoyance: Dani. Those ignored texts and canceled plans had caught up with me. Her arms crossed over her chest, a backpack on. She let herself in, pushing past me and immediately going up the stairs. "What, you couldn't be bothered to answer a single text? You can't *possibly* be that busy." She didn't wait for my response as she walked up the steps, turning into my bedroom before I had closed the front door. I took a deep breath, extremely not in the mood for this, or anything, actually. I just wanted to watch a movie in my pj's.

*"Not when you're not native to the language and don't encounter it daily, actually, I'm happy to report."* Sia's reply was delayed; maybe it was some form of courtesy so I didn't have to listen to more than one conversation at once. Or maybe it was Sia trying to figure out Dani's emotions as well, if Sia was truly my *future self*, as she claimed, and therefore had this empathy thing too. I had no idea, but the momentary silence had been blissful.

"Kind of have been," I said as I walked up the stairs. "It's been... hectic."

"Hectic with *what*? Finals aren't for another month at your school. *I checked.*" For maybe the first time ever, I was thankful to not share a school district with Dani, herself being across county lines despite us living within walking distance of each other. I'd always wanted us to be in class together, something that hadn't been possible since we met at daycare years back.

"I, um." It wasn't something I was comfortable talking about. Even less so to Dani, who refused to acknowledge there had been any change, as even the current conversation indicated. "Just... a lot."

A further spike of annoyance and... something I couldn't identify. Something negative, bad, hostile. Could've been from anyone in the room, or well, around me better said given most of the individuals around didn't have a physical presence. I assumed it was from Dani though, given that Sia and Kisate's conversation had been the standard back and forth. "Not *this* again."

*"You aren't even creating spells in their native language,"* obviously, *so your general competency on foundation is debatable at best,"* Kisate said. And here *they* went yet again, too.

*"At least I can create and not just mindlessly spit out whatever's on a spell book page. Spells aren't inherently based on a specific language. Sure, Riyatian was structured to have additional support metrics for certain aspects with spells, especially in modifiers, but —"*

I wasn't that interested in what Sia said, but having multiple conversations going on at once was overwhelming, and I had accidentally blanked on replying to Dani because to me, there had yet to be a lapse in silence. "Hello? Why are you just standing there?"

"Sorry," I said. Too much was going on. Felt like six people were talking all over each other at once. That wasn't actually the case — only three people talked and only one had a physical presence, but the stark contrast of emotions led to what could only be described as sensory noise, not something I could tangibly point out but there. "I just... today isn't good, okay? I don't know when will be. I wish I did. I'm sorry you came all this way, but I can't."

Regardless of if I believed my life to be in danger, I had two angry voices in my head demanding that I learn an entire other culture, an entire other language, an entire other *system* that I didn't know existed a month and a half ago.

"You keep saying that." Louder annoyance, this aggression ebbing into my mind; I winced as my heart rate increased, my muscles tensing as a flush rose to my cheeks. I wasn't angry. I wasn't annoyed. But my body reacted like it was, and that made everything even more disorienting to where I wanted to lash out, but wasn't sure at what I was even lashing at. "You say there's *other voices* or whatever, but I've never seen them. And I bet *he* hasn't either, because if I haven't, *he* definitely wouldn't have." Ironically, Jordan was the only one who *had* actually met any of the voices in my head: he said he met Sia on the day things happened. I remember nothing past the words Sia had me say so had no idea if he was lying or not, but there wasn't really a reason for him to lie about it, not in the hushed whisper he'd had when he asked if I was all right that Monday morning in homeroom.

Moreover... what did Dani want from me? That one of them would spontaneously take over my body and have coffee with her? I couldn't project their voices to others, long would've if I could. I could say I had other voices in my mind, could say *something* obviously saved us that day, could say emotions overwhelmed my very being right then. But I couldn't physically prove any of it to Dani. Wasn't sure I believed it myself, some *reincarnated princess* from a *destroyed magic kingdom* and could *use magic*. Sounded like something out of a fantasy book. Not even an original one. Cliche almost. And yet.

Yet.

It didn't matter if it sounded far-fetched, if it sounded stupid: it was the only explanation I had been given. Something that attacked who I was, had always believed I was. Wasn't being in honors track enough? Wasn't maintaining my GPA the thing that was supposed to secure my future?

*"How is she supposed to revive Riyati, as is her duty, if — "* Kisate snapped.

I wanted none of it. Wanted away. No more noise, no more responsibilities, no more demands and throbbing pain in my head and trying to juggle multiple conversations that I had no agency in or answers to or *anything*.

There was black. Dani wasn't there anymore, and this vast darkness had replaced my room. Glancing around, I saw others in this blackness — girls with hair the same color as my own and eyes almost the same, something I didn't even share with Mom.

One of the girls, the one with long hair in a long ponytail, rolled her eyes. "Of *course* she rushes away to the body."

The body? Where was I? Where was Dani?

Another girl appeared between me and the girl who had spoken — her body was partially translucent. Long hair to her hips, reddish-brown like the others. She leaned her weight on her left side, left hand on her hip. "You'd rather have needless injuries? Wasn't seeing you exactly take charge with those *refined* instincts of yours." That was Sia. Full stop. But how?

Another of the girls — one who hadn't spoken so far — rolled her eyes as well and mumbled something under her breath. She pointed toward me before motioning to come closer. I did so, leading that girl to put her hand over mine as the blackness covered my vision. I should've panicked, but at least there was silence. The silence didn't last long before the same girl was beside me once more, accompanied by another who looked the closest to me in age of the ones I had seen so far.

"They're not stoppin' anytime soon."

Leah. It was Leah, a distinct roughness to her dialect that I hadn't heard from any of the other *incarnations*. How was I seeing them? Where was this? "I don't..." What should I even ask? Was I dead somehow? Disconnected from my body, judging by —

It just clicked: that first voice — the first girl — had been Kisate. That meant this other girl that hadn't spoken yet was Chloé. Didn't lessen the confusion about how any of this was going on, though at least I wasn't in danger. Maybe.

There was a pulse, a sense of pride. Emotions — I was still picking up on them? But how? Shy and eager and hope and pride and irritation all interwove around me. Less than what I felt from Dani, but more than the normally muted expressions from the others within me. Chloé walked forward, hugging me around the neck. "It's okay." That would've been more comforting if I didn't have a midterm worth of questions that I needed answered.

"Y'know where ya at?" Leah asked. I shook my head, somewhat limited by Chloé yet to let go. "Thought so. Makes it impressive as hell. She might actually be onto somethin' after all." The latter part was more of mumbled under Leah's breath but not quiet enough that I couldn't make out the words. "It's a subcon — subconscious principality. Think like the inside of your brain. Most people cannot access theirs w'out a hell'va lotta trainin' though. How you tapped it anyway's hell'va impressive actually."

Those were words. Not words that I understood, but I nodded anyway, pretending like it made any sense at all. I got the fact that somehow, Leah and Chloé, and in the previous blackness, Kisate and Sia, had been their own *people*. Some type of verification that the voices in my mind were *real*. But then... where was Dani? How would I get back? And why had Kisate and Sia disappeared? "The other two — that was Kisate and Sia right? But they disappeared?"

"Leah did that!" Chloé chirped her response, as if she had just clarified everything. It, in fact, clarified barely anything, but there was a warmth to Chloé's emotions that was comforting compared to the harshness of Kisate. I had assumed that Kisate was too loud, blocking out the others. But that actually didn't make sense given that Sia's mouth at least wasn't exactly quiet by any definition. To be fair, though, Sia was supposedly also the one adjusting the amount of empathy I felt from others, so maybe she could manipulate that to hide her own emotions. Or maybe Kisate was truly that emotionally "loud" compared to the others, where she was quiet compared to other individuals outside my mind but certainly the loudest within it.

Point being, Chloé didn't have the aggression of Kisate. Was calm, a gentle happiness, and I really needed that right then.

"You did?" I asked.

Leah nodded, crossing her arms as she leaned back, as if against a wall. What wall, I had no idea, but it supported her somehow. "Since we got individual minds, have our own subcons still. Yours act as the 'joint space' since's linked to a physical body."

*That* was how Kisate walled herself off every night. Why did she get to hide while I was stuck, never having a second alone? Taking in the surrounding space, I saw blackness as before — the blackness I'd created somehow, according to Leah. Unlike the first one, though, this one had a few cracks, hairline. I wasn't sure how I could even see it since it was like broken glass, reflective and smooth and *black*, but somehow broken in just a few spots. I would've easily missed it had one not been right beside me. I kneeled, running my pointer finger over it, noticing the sliver felt like cracked glass but had not cut my finger. "What's this?"

"Ah, it's. Dun worry 'bout it. Just shit that's in the past."

Something from the past? I had noticed this too quickly for something like it to have been in my own *subcon*. I wasn't asking further though, given Leah clearly didn't want to talk about it. "Thank you, for taking me from um. Before. And away from Dani."

"You did that actually," Chloe said. "I think you're the first since Kisate — well, excluding Sia, she seems to come and go as easily as Kisate. But you're the first who's figured out how to enter one while alive. Leah and me never did. Really surprised us actually. Probably would've given yourself a nasty bruise though since no one was in control of your body when you did it, kinda renders it unconscious if no soul's in control." As if realizing how that might be a concerning statement to me, Chloé moved her hands back and forth rapidly. "Sia immediately took over though before you'd even fully found your way to your subcon. How she's able to maintain conscious control and project even a fraction of inner representation is insane though, like. I don't even think Kisate could do that."

"Don't say that too loud," Leah said, a bit of a grumble in her voice. "We won't hear the damn end of it for the next three years. An' I'm not sold on 'Sia' hearin' it either." Exasperation. That was the grumble, the feeling dominating this "room." It wasn't just me sick and tired of their nonstop squabbles a month into us all being stuck together. However, it raised the question that kept repeating over and over:

If Sia truly was myself years from now, why did I feel more mature than Sia? Why was Sia picking fights? I knew I wasn't always passive, but I certainly wasn't out to argue with people either. Meanwhile, Sia and Kisate couldn't have three words before going at each other, and most of the time, Sia was the one who started it.

If Sia was me, what had happened?

# Chapter Five

## special

As I opened the heavy wooden classroom door, I felt dozens of eyes on me, including my homeroom teacher who paused whatever he'd been saying. I lowered my head from the attention as I softly closed the door back and made my way to my seat. Five damn minutes wasn't even that much. "That's the fourth time this quarter, Mr. Boyle. Next time is detention."

"Yessir." Wasn't like it's actually my fault I'm late. Thomas couldn't find the bag with his clothes in it from the move, and I got stuck helping him since Jewel'd already bailed and Elaine's hung over; hell knew she ain't moving for at least the next three hours since she'd been puking when I got up this morning.

Kylie didn't notice me sit down beside her, intently focused on writing something; she's prob'bly the only one in the damn class that didn't, too accustomed to me being late to every damn thing. Given so many of our classmates were like Kylie and shared classes with me since elementary, I'd long given up on them not caring. As had been the case for years, there're hushed giggles and whispers as classmates glanced my way none too subtly. I lowered my head further, eyes resting on the blank notebook page Kylie's scribbling on. For once, it ain't her

29

planner out; she always reviewed shit and actually wrote down upcoming events in there. Was it homework? Wasn't like her to be trying to do shit this late; it'd always been me trying to sneak something in last minute, not her. I shifted my weight to get a better glance; she sat on my right and was left-handed, so wasn't hard to see what had her focus. There's an intent glare on her face as her nose scrunched up, completely entranced. On the paper, there're dots and circles and lines — like a code. Nothing I'd seen her write b'fore. She'd never been an especially artistic person either, often complaining in any arts classes we had back in elementary and running away from them once she could. Made zero sense, but she'd rather have an additional academic class over any electives, and for the life of me, I'd never understood volunteering for more damn homework. Point being, I seriously doubted she'd suddenly found a new calling as a Morse Code artist.

"Shut up," she said under her breath.

Ah, so that's what it was: more of the so-called "training" she'd mentioned had eaten every damn free second. School's usually a "safe zone" away from it. "What's that?"

She jumped before closing her eyes and releasing a breath I didn't even know she'd been holding. "Sorry, was, um, distracted."

Understatement of the year. "Looked like it, yeah."

"Um." Her pencil lowered, giving a gentle push to the notebook that moved it closer to me. "There's a whole other language, writing system included. Was trying to practice a bit because the characters are weird, like *this* is their alphabet somehow. And there's also a peanut gallery that could really learn when to let people practice in *peace*." Yet another time I looked to be part of a conversation I might as well've not been in the room for; people assumed she was talking to me instead of the voices that'd been there since that day a month ago. It was confusing as fuck to keep up with, but I didn't mind being a cover, was something I could help with. Still would've been nice to know the hell's going on though, 'specially times like this when I *was* part of the conversation but randomly forgotten.

I tilted my head to get a better view of the page. "What's it say?"

"Nothing. Just like... random letters, basically. Not even in order. As I have now been *very* informed." Kylie'd always been *exceptional*. Top of the class, all honors. Excelled at everything. Had a loving mother who cared too much as her worst fault, had lived in the same house the whole time I'd known her, maybe even her whole life. I knew the way to her house better than the past four places I'd lived combined.

For not the first time, I wondered why someone that so naturally lit up a room's around someone like me. That she's more special than we'd known, that she could use *magic* and was learning at the rate that it consumed so much of her time, wasn't really that surprising; she'd always had eyes on her, and I preferred it that way; if people focused on her, then I could be in the background. For once, I could just be not noticed, not the one everyone kept whispering 'bout and around. Not the one the teachers saw as a disappointment-in-training, waiting to end up in prison or on welfare. Well. Continued welfare, given my whole family already's on subsidized damn near everything and still couldn't — whatever. "Which one's it this time?"

"Kisate. Whole thing is Kisate's very won't shut up about it tangent. It's not fair that Sia outright *left* and just went to bed and I'm stuck suffering because of it." A brief pause before she said, "Yes, I know you can hear me. I just don't even care anymore."

Sia. The only one I had met and even then, only briefly, maybe minutes at most. She'd saved my life somehow. All our lives. Kisate's the oldest, I'd gathered that much, and she and Sia had bitch fights a lot. That was the extent I understood any of the voices, though, outside of just knowing that were more than those two. "They sleep?"

"Yes. And should do so *significantly more*, just throwing it out there." Dani and me were the only other ones that knew 'bout these other voices; Kylie hadn't told anyone else. Like some exclusive club, something I shouldn't have been aware of. She prob'bly wouldn't have even told either of us if we hadn't been there when shit went down. It'd been one month since that day, and it seemed so long ago yet wasn't at all. Hell, it'd happened like a week after my birthday. Yet another day of bullshit outside of the necklace Kylie'd gotten me, a black rope chain with this strange pendant that's a black circle with a cut out of a triangle inside it. She'd said wasn't sure why, but it just really reminded her of me. Had even been uncharacteristically awkward, like she's scared of offending me, prob'bly 'cause it's jewelry and admittedly's kinda awkward to get. But as happened every year, didn't really care what she got me 'cause it's more than my family did; we didn't even bother saying happy birthday to each other since there's fuck-all money to do shit with regardless. I always expected this to be the year she finally forgot, and it had yet to happen, the date being in her planner like every other damn thing under the sun.

The bell rang for class change; she huffed, her brilliant aquamarine eyes meeting mine for a moment. "I can't believe I'm *excited* for math at 8:30 *in the morning*." Morning complaints from her were hardly new. I might've been the one always late, but she's the one that'd always hated mornings; most of my energy'd always hit right as the sun rose while as much as she hated mornings, I'm surprised she didn't chug coffee just to make it to the classroom before noon. "My life's reached a new low." I chuckled at her complaint as I picked up my backpack — hadn't ever bothered to unzip it in the first place, 'specially not given the damn zipper kept getting jammed. I needed to sew a new one. Again.

She was already out of the classroom before I even stood, and I felt the edges of my smile fade. Was the last person I'd talk to 'til lunch when I'd see her again. She's my only friend, the only one who ever wanted to get to know me and talk with me and didn't see me as below her, even if I absolutely was.

# Chapter Six

# history lessons

It was hour three of *Riyatian history lessons*. I wasn't a particular fan of academic subjects in general, but history was hanging out around math in my least favorite list: what date and what name and it all just blurred together. It was over, in the past, already happened. Who cared?

Yet if I had any shot of enjoying my Sunday — or even getting some of my *actual* study prep for this year's finals — , I had a good hour or two left of Kisate monologuing, going on and on and *on*. If Sia went back to bed while Kisate was lecturing again, I was going to — . Well. I actually didn't know of anything I could do to Sia. But I wished I did because it was not *fair* to leave me helpless and stuck with Kisate. Sia was strict, sarcastic, and merciless, but at least her rambling had the vaguest sense of practicality. I really wasn't sure what the point of learning three ancestors up of Kisate's family line was; they were all dead. Forgotten. And very not going to be on my geography final next month.

Holding my left hand open, I focused on the only actual tangible "magic" they'd taught me: a small light that illuminated from my palm. Moving my thumb away from the

33

light, I extended the same light a third of an inch more. It still was amazing that *I* had created this ball of light, something about manipulating the air with reflection and something else. I zoned out on the actual logistics because at the end of the day, what I cared about was *I made light.* Why couldn't I learn something more like this? Something I could show or do, something that was tangible and real and —

*"Are you even listening to me?"* Kisate asked, and I felt like that kid in class who had a ruler smacked on my hand. The obvious answer was no, not at all; I clocked out at least fifteen minutes prior to generating my magic fidget toy of an illuminated orb. I knew better than to admit that, though.

"Yeah, you were talking about um... the Riyati royal line..." Wasn't my most convincing cover, but I needed a break, and Kisate had already said she didn't care and was continuing until she decided I *deserved* a break.

*"I was not. I was speaking about the Tanoti line, which had diverged from the Riyati line at least three generations prior to Her Majesty's, that is, my mother's, rule. Furthermore —"*

*"Mm. I have a question,"* Sia said. So she *was* awake. I hadn't been able to sense her, but that wasn't exactly unusual — Kisate and Sia were both able to block themselves off rather efficiently; Sia could somehow remain aware while doing so, while Kisate didn't care if she missed something. I didn't know what god to thank that Chloé and Leah were both more reserved with imposing onto my life, but that god needed a weekly tribute. *"So, how'd the great Riyatian family tree collapse again?"*

*"How dare you."* That was the first time Kisate had ever *not* wanted to talk about the apparently-great Riyatian royal family, and the reaction alone got me a bit curious about the subject.

*"I think it's a valid question. A rather pressing one even. You want me to start? I know this one pretty well."* Sia not backing down was rather common, but there was something more going on in this conversation. I wasn't sure what, but this wasn't just Kisate and Sia's normal spats. There was a deep... sadness, fear even, like a wave of longing that made me want to reach for childhood stuffed toys to hold. These feelings had to be from Kisate: Chloé was still asleep as far as I could tell, it

being her usual afternoon nap time, and the faintly cautious emotion made more sense for Leah. Sia was blank, as usual.

*"All she needs to know is that she is to restart Riyati. She is to do as I was entrusted and preserve the bloodline with the Kaku Tiza."*

*"How?"* Sia's question was so pointed, so confident, that *I* could tell Sia knew the answer. There was something between the two of them that was very unsaid, and neither one wanted to flat out state whatever they implied. The fact that there were things left unsaid terrified me considering both had said less than pleasant things with little to no resistance multiple times already. A second passed before Sia spoke again. *"Let's explain what 'Kaku Tiza' is since you've neglected that in all your family lines so far; you didn't even break the translation down. And what obstacles are in the way of your mentioned goal? A rather pressing one, I'd say. All because* you *couldn't be bothered to tell him 'no' back in the day. Fascinating stuff, way more interesting than your great uncle."*

*"Sia, that's enough,"* Leah said, her voice firm, like she was disciplining a child. To be fair, that was typically exactly how I would normally describe Sia and Kisate's spats. Not this time, though.

*"No. It's not."* There was a quiet fury in Sia's tone. A lack of the collected, detached control that had been there prior. *"She will never be 'Kisate Riyati.' Could never be. You're setting up for false expectations and are going to stand around acting like it wasn't what killed yourself and Chloé. I refuse. I won't spare her feelings at the cost of the things I care about."*

Wait, Leah and Chloé were killed by Kisate? Kisate was demanding and prissy and condescending and a ton of other problematic things, but she wasn't a killer.

"I don't..." I said.

Leah said nothing. Kisate said nothing.

Sia scoffed. *"You always leave the dirty work to other people so you don't have to deal with it. Fine. I'll say it: Kisate let her servant boy think he had a chance because she couldn't be bothered to reject him. She was already engaged — that's the 'Kaku Tiza,' or 'High Prince,' Tanoti line she was talking about, and her fiancé was also one of the few who got reincarnated. Fun fact, she's made* damn *sure to force you into emulating her path there. Back to said servant boy, he obviously hated Kisate's fiancé, and was none too pleased to find out about the reincarnation spell. Leads us to today, where we're stuck dealing with him* relieving *Kisate of having to be with the Kaku Tiza line by murdering the current incarnation. He's succeeded twice so far. I'd really rather third time not be the charm."*

What?

I had no words. Fiancé? Arranged marriage?

Someone I'd never even met wanted to kill me because of a guy I didn't know existed prior to a few minutes ago and didn't even want a relationship with. I wanted to go to college, not waste time in lovers' quarrels. Couldn't I just say that? It was all a misunderstanding.

Everything was a misunderstanding.

Kisate finally spoke once more: *"He cares, always has. Just... doesn't understand what he thinks best isn't..."*

*"And your indecisiveness has trapped Leah and Chloé here. So, thanks for that."* Sia winced with the last few words, a flash of pain shooting through me. A raw anger that sent my heart racing, consuming. Sia had slipped somehow, and even that moment of her normally hidden emotions had me almost unable to swallow. *"Damn it, not now."* Her tone was strained.

"Sia?" Something slammed into my shoulder; I winced as I glanced down. No one and nothing. Not even red irritation, which definitely should've been there given it felt like my whole front shoulder had been hit.

A deep sigh — that boiling rage slipped into frustration and sadness and helplessness. Sia hadn't resumed hiding her own emotions; it was the first time I experienced them. *"For some reason — even I don't know why —, I... we, you. Have two abilities. First is empathy, which you've experienced to some degree."* How Sia kept her voice steady, I wasn't sure. I felt my wrist be gripped, skin rubbing and pinched. Nothing. Nothing was there. *"The second is a form of clairvoyance: sensory precognition. Feeling the future. How far out you can feel will increase with increased magipoten — increased mana."*

*"Wait."* Leah spoke, this sudden panic — like a mild terror — flashing through her voice. I thought she was the one that caused the stomach dropping sensation I had, but it was hard to separate anything out with so much going on, multiple sets of

36

emotions and my own pain and why did I feel my wrist was getting squeezed so hard I should've had bruises?

*"She's relaying through me. Can't pick up something to this intensity on her own. That's why there's a delay and I'm able to buffer it still."* Sia was somehow preventing some of this *sensory precognition*. That's why I could feel her emotions and even this pain. Yet Sia's words hadn't soothed Leah at all: another unspoken exchange. Kisate had not spoken again after her earlier meek defense. *"Sleep it off, Kylie. I'll have it managed when you wake up."* Right as I went to protest, the pain from each emotion and invisible-hit increased to where I momentarily saw spots in my vision.

Sia wasn't ordering me; she gave me an escape. This was an act of kindness. My eyes watered as *something* hit the same shoulder from earlier while it was still sensitive from the previous impact. I stumbled to my bed, crashing to the mattress and pillow without bothering to pull the blankets up over me.

The world went blissfully black.

# Chapter Seven

## around and around

Siani | April 29
Rae Residence

My old friend the ceiling fan was back. Around and around and around. Yet again, a too apt description of my life.

My younger self would easily be unconscious the rest of the night if not days; that attack was something she wouldn't have picked up on her own for another few years at least. I needed to do better. Be better. But I screwed up, letting my emotions cloud judgment long enough that not only did I pick up on this attack, but she did as well by getting a read off myself. All I could do now was wait the attack out, taking the brunt of the body's physiological strain until this passed.

I hated I knew what this attack was, and there was absolutely nothing I could do to lessen the pain. For either of them.

Kisate ran away as soon as my younger self blacked out. Chloé had woken up in the middle of our argument but knew better than to say anything and instead retreated to her own subcon as fast as she subtly could. Brought up another question actually: what *did* the dead do for hours on end? The mental exertion requiring a period of processing made sense, which was effectively what their "sleep" was — a period of brain inactivity allowing for preservation and emotional processing. But there was no physical energy to burn; that was only something a physical body had. No wonder going insane was so easy for them — boredom was more of a valid concern than I had realized until my current position, and my position was still significantly different given how active of a role I had.

A throb to my wrist. Here we freaking go again. Must've been the third round, was most definitely the same attack. No doubt, the pain would've woken my younger self up if she had active control right then. Was better that I dealt with it.

I knew a thing or two about pain, after all.

*"Sia?"* Leah asked.

Go figure. I knew Leah was up and hadn't run away like the other two, but given how unamused she was at the whole episode, I figured at least a few days before she'd remotely acknowledge me. She wasn't suddenly feeling friendlier either, could completely verify that among the other thirty-something emotions I was picking up on. Why were town homes so close together? Yard space. Or, well, empath reading space, but still. "Mm?" I could've gone through the typical effort of splitting my consciousness, but it was harder when I couldn't place Kylie in quasi-control and split the mental and sensory processing; there was a lot I got away with by knowing how to be creative with the resources I had and the limits of myself and my younger self down to a very precise technical level.

*"There had'ta be a better way than that."* Leah wasn't wrong: there almost certainly was. I knew I had more than a few unresolved feelings toward Kisate in particular, and that snuck out a bit. ...Well, more than a bit actually: snaps that weren't necessary; fights that weren't worth fighting.

"It needed to be said."

*"Like that? Seriously the best timin' all that 'future knowledge' could manage?"*

The moon shone in through the open blinds; was one of the few movements I had made after my younger self went unconscious because it comforted me, reminded me of all the times I had spent alone in my room, trying to think through my choices and fears. Missed the absence of company right then, or at least the absence of my current company.

There was no point in lying; Leah would see through it,

especially since I wasn't exactly in top form from my — Kylie's — body aching with the hits felt through the premonition as it was.

I was tired, missed home right then.

"It's not like my memory is perfect. I remember broad strokes, but I don't remember what I ate for breakfast four years ago, sorry. But I do know this insistence of Kisate that everything must be taught exactly how she learned it, that trying to force 'us' to be 'her,' is going lead to another dead incarnation. You learn dead relative trees in peace, not war." I paused, but Leah didn't fill in the silence. After a few minutes, I added, "We're the only ones that have killed people. And no, that's not something I put together as the child you're used to. It's something you realize when you interact with someone, and they're watching every movement, anticipating the next movement and what exits are in every environment. Kisate and Chloé didn't have to kill to survive. It's on me, and I can't operate on delusions and wasted time. I don't have the luxury."

*"Kisate means well. And hiding all your plans ain't exactly makin' it easy to trust you, 'specially after today's outburst."*

"I know." I didn't need them to trust me; I just needed them to behave to my expectations, and they had yet to fail. Kisate had to assert her identity over the others: she *owned* us, by virtue of being the "original." Chloé was the peacekeeper, wanting things to be frictionless, just for everyone to get along without realizing the cost of passivity. Leah would monitor my every movement, but she wouldn't act unless she felt her hand forced. This confrontation was as far as Leah would go.

Knowing the future wasn't my biggest strength; it was just my selling pitch to their initial trust.

That said, Leah was correct: I needed better restraint. Couldn't feel lonely. Couldn't feel scared. Couldn't indulge the anger that likely would never leave.

*"Will you apologize at least?"*

"How do you feel — when she says you *don't exist*? That's fine?" Of course it wasn't. It ruffled both Leah and Chloé each time, just like it did me and my younger self.

*"It's just... how she is."*

I closed my eyes. Kisate had won in ways I would likely always hate. I wanted to rebel and fight to the death. But I

**41**

couldn't. "This is just how I am as well. What makes Kisate herself is also what makes me myself, so I refuse to shelter her further. Fact is, Asuza won't leave Kylie alone once he realizes who she is. We know he has bounties out, and that based on how things went with Chloé, he's getting more efficient each time."

Leah paused, though for only a few seconds. She didn't want to admit I had a point, but I did, and we both knew it. *"What's theory and what's memory in this?"*

As ever, I couldn't answer that. It wasn't worth the risk. "Who's to say."

# Chapter Eight

## just another day

There's a loud crash from out in the kitchenette. A bang? Might've been Thomas rummaging through his clothes bags. Was s'posed to have been sorting out what we needed for the laundry mat later, but hell knew he prob'bly got distracted yet again. I'd been attempting to scrub out a stain in the carpet, but mixing alcohol with a different type of alcohol only succeeded in giving me a headache. Was a miracle everything we owned didn't reek. Jewel's s'posed to be the one stuck on trash duty, so could've been her dropping one of the glass bottles too. Or maybe Elaine's knock-out drunk again and crashed while opening the door.

"Damn fuckin' — "

I swallowed, felt my body tense. It's the one thing I hadn't tried to predict 'cause I wished it'd been any of those things over this. Anything but *that* tone from my father. Thomas whimpered. He knew too. I felt Thomas's eyes move toward me. Heard more banging, something thrown against the wall — it shattered.

Dammit, Jewel hadn't picked up all the beer bottles fast enough, prob'bly had been picking cans up too but those didn't leave shards for the next month, was why bottles were the damn priority. Had been nice not dealing with damn glass for a few weeks since this place didn't have that problem yet. Three weeks might've even been a record.

My hands shook ever so slightly, a tremble I hated; the intensity increased as I heard another slam into the wall: my father threw something.

"D-dad, what happened?" Jewel asked. The usual bossiness of her voice was gone. Panic, that slight quiver and softness and slower words. "I thought you went to go get — "

"They ain't letting me buy the damn thing I went for. Said it's Sunday, but fuck that, I's there then and ain't going back." He's going back later, no doubt. Not for groceries like he'd claimed, but more beer as usual. Would've been more surprising if he actually bought something else; that's one of Elaine's consistent chores and, to the surprise of us all, she's actually reliable with it. Prob'bly 'cause she worked there anyways and didn't get to eat either if we had nothing here.

Another thing thrown. He's furious at a rule that'd been in place longer than he'd prob'bly been alive. Couldn't buy alcohol before noon on Sundays.

I did my best to sneak into the room and start picking things up behind him b'fore he injured himself and got even more pissed. I winced as my finger pricked glass, blood rising to the incision point. My father turned from Jewel, where he'd been waving his arms, to noticing me.

Fuck.

"You damn good f'nothings, all I wanted's something good for once." I smelt alcohol still on my father's breath, saw even more glass in the box with our kitchen plastic cups and plates that's still by the front door, yet to be unpacked. Saw the hole in the sheetrock between the front door and the bathroom — would need to patch that later with wherever the hell the paste-shit was.

Then felt pain — sharp, electric almost, sending a buzz through my nerves and up to my head. My father punched my shoulder, throbbing shooting out from that one spot across to the other shoulder. Grabbed my wrist b'fore throwing me to the brown fake laminate flooring and kicking me. Jewel did her best to be small, blend into the boxes, stay out of sight. Thomas stayed in our shared room; I made out an occasional hiccup.

This's why Elaine never wanted to come home; partied and slept around and I only wished I did the same, had friends to run away to, someone that actually wanted my ass.

Another kick. Balled fist slamming down on my shoulder. Would have to wear long-sleeved shirts again despite it basically being May and hot as hell and humid and.

Fuck. Another kick, breath knocked out of me right as I'd started feeling air in my lungs.

I tightened my eyes, wincing with each blow. At knowing there's nothing I could do. At just wanting and waiting and *begging* for this to end, for my father to leave and pass out drunk somewhere.

There're only two modes for my father: violence and semi-sober or drunk and unconscious.

Like every time past, I pleaded for the latter to happen quicker, 'specially as I tightened my eyes upon feeling glass slice my cheek.

Just another day.

# Chapter Nine

# ice-blue eyes

It had been a while since I sat at a high school desk, barely remembered which was mine at this point, and I had thoroughly erased how uncomfortable the stupid things were. At least my organizational strategies rather thankfully had shifted little over the years, so after skimming through the planner and already finished homework, I mentally organized how to be "Kylie" for the day, or at least until my younger self woke up. I wasn't expecting much until at least noon if she had been out all since late Saturday afternoon: the strain of everything caused her to collapse, and I wasn't really that surprised.

I saw Jordan sneak in right with the homeroom teacher — what even was the teacher's name again? Wasn't really important, but still. Tenth grade seemed like another lifetime, and I didn't realize it until confronted with the *mundaneness* of it. My eyes followed Jordan: scrape on left cheek, backpack favoring left side when he was right-handed, long sleeve shirt and baggy jeans on. Before he'd hit the school grounds, I'd already picked up the sour emotions and pain radiating off him; I had fully expected and braced for them, knew it had been

47

coming. His eyes were distant: his body was there, but his mind certainly wasn't. There was no light, only a tunnel.

"Hanging in there?" I asked, my voice hushed so as not to attract attention.

"Yeah." His voice was soft, his mind distant; he dropped his backpack onto the cream tile flooring as he sat down.

Minutes passed in silence; he wasn't in a mood to talk, and we were supposed to be paying attention to the morning announcements. Neither of us were, but then again, I would be surprised if most of the class wasn't ignoring said morning announcements: they'd repeat right as the day ended, through an email to student email, to parents, and probably with physical fliers for the big things. Students weren't exactly encouraged to listen closely. I definitely couldn't blame the students I saw smuggling phones in their desk cubbies, texting someone, or the notes getting passed around if they were near to a friend. I had been that student more than once, something my younger self had yet to experience.

Not soon enough, the announcements finished, leaving idle gossip for the rest of homeroom. Jordan hadn't even unpacked his bag, resting his forehead on the desk. His head still throbbed, echoed throughout my own. Was as *emotionally loud* as ever.

There were signs so obvious that I wouldn't realize for years. "I can help, if you want," I said as I placed the planner back into the backpack and zipped said backpack for the next destination: lovely math, where I could calculate if x was in front of me, how quickly could I slam my head into the desk and end my suffering. Well. Not now, actually: that'd give Kylie a headache when she woke back up *and* wouldn't be productive to basically any of my goals.

I moved my eyes to him, watching him sit up from where he had been resting. "Huh?"

How to even approach this? I knew it was a sensitive subject. But leaving him in pain wasn't an option. Couldn't be. For a lot of reasons, really. I lowered my eyes from him to my now empty desk. "She — Kylie. She's asleep right now. I'm the one you met that day, Sia." Actually, thinking about it, that dumb mage really pissed me off: she was obviously trapping people to siphon mana off of and then killing them once she'd done so. Mages had enough problems as it was without her adding to them.

Ice-blue eyes widened as he sat up. "What? Is she...?"

"Oh, just fatigued." Fatigued from a sensory precognition attack pain overload, but technical details; my younger self could use the time to mentally process anyways. There weren't many breaks I could give her, but I also knew she could only learn so quickly. "Am just covering for her, basically."

Relief, a slight exhale from where he held breath without realizing it. Was so adorable to see; I had to bite back a chuckle. "Ah, uh. Thank you, for that day."

"Mm. It's nothing." It was weird for our conversation to be so stilted. Maybe I should've lied, not said who I was. He likely wouldn't have been able to tell the difference since he had only met *Sia* once so far. "You remember that day, how you weren't hurt anymore after everything?"

"Y-yeah. Was amazing, like nothing ever happened."

"You nee — ." I couldn't be that direct, not right then. Had been almost natural for a moment. "I know you're hurt." His hand flinched, eyes widened as he backed away ever so slightly. "I know what happened. I won't ask questions or tell her. Just... let me take care of it, like I did that day."

The bell rang; students rushed out with the teacher not far behind them. Jordan and I were among the few stragglers left.

His lower lip trembled. "But... how?"

I put my finger over my lips. I couldn't say. That was something for him to discover, not for me to share. "The future isn't mine to tell. But the present, I can help with."

*"Why is he injured?"* That was the first thing Kisate had said since running away to her own subcon Saturday. *"What happened — this level of healing magic...?"*

Kisate had correctly noticed that I had summoned just a bit of mana, placing my hand over his bare hand and moving both inside the desk to mask the aura generation from the spell. While I could repress auras on mild healing magic, I unfortunately needed a modification of the spell to not need direct contact with the injury — there were too many spots to otherwise make it practical in the limited time and open space. The cut on his cheek faded into a scar, head calmed, and his shoulder was no longer inflamed. There might've been a fractured rib too, but I wasn't paying enough attention to verify there. *"Siani —"* It was the first time Kisate addressed me by name in the month and a half we'd been stuck together. *"He's — how did you know? How did you know when we never noticed?"*

*"Sorry, but that's not true."* Unlike Saturday evening when I could talk aloud, that wasn't an option in this near-empty classroom; I needed to create the link to reply from the subcon, which was annoying, but whatever. *"I'm not the only one who knew. Just the only one who stepped in to take care of it."*

# Chapter Ten

## protection

Owing to how *terrible* the week had been, Sia and Kisate weren't even demanding my entire weekend like normal. I vaguely wondered if it was because they'd barely spoken to each other since last week. For the first time since they invaded my brain, sometimes there had been *hours* that passed in silence. Brief respites where I could try to forget the past nearing two-months ever happened, only one conversation going on around me. Unfortunately, I still felt the emotions of people nearby, so there were reminders that March hadn't been a dream. There had been far fewer intense emotions from the others occupying my body — definitely nothing from Sia since that one day —, but those *around me* just became more present in exchange, and it had kind of sucked. That was why I bit my lip, feeling *something* from the redhead beside me. Something I couldn't place was intense and I didn't dare bring it up. As it was, guilt compelled me to let Dani know I had a free weekend for a sleepover. But I didn't want to spend it with her, even if it was just Friday and Saturday, and we were even going to my house for once.

What had happened to where I felt *annoyed* with Dani just

wanting to hang out? Sleepovers were distant now, something so casual that I couldn't relate to anymore. There was this disconnect between us now that hadn't been there prior to mid-March; it had been growing greater and greater, and it was now unfortunately right in the metaphorical middle of my face because of the silence from those in my head: Sia wasn't making remarks, Kisate wasn't lecturing about something absolutely boring, Chloé wasn't trying to work in idle friendly chatter, and Leah wasn't... well, Leah had always been the quietest one, actually.

"And I told him, absolutely not. Thought he had a *chance*; he can't even get into an AP class. Pathetic," Dani said.

"Y-yeah." I didn't even know what she was talking about. Just that Dani was getting very riled up by it, and *that* was now my problem; it hadn't even been a week since the *sensory precognition attack,* as Sia had called it. Despite Sia uncharacteristically being generous and actually giving me time to rest, my physical body had not received that kindness, and I felt it so much right then. First, Sia had stayed up all that night and it might've even gone into Sunday. Either way, my physical body had been exhausted by the time my consciousness woke up on Monday. I hadn't rested all week between catching up on actual school I hadn't gotten to during the weekend and then the Monday classes I had missed. Even worse, the atmosphere had been *tense* the entire week, and that was even more emotional strain on me.

In short: my body was exhausted, and my brain wasn't much better. But Dani had been desperate and near begging for things to be *normal again*, so I felt an obligation to text her I'd be free.

I really hated that lapse in judgment, even if it was *the right thing* to do.

"This's why we should be in the same school — it's so dumb that they redistricted *again* and still didn't fix that." Something about Dani's emotions was *suffocating*. It wasn't like how *loud* Jordan was without ever saying a word, or how my mother was over-protective. Actually, there was something similar with Dani and Jordan, but —

*"Mm, go left, not right,"* Sia said. Right was toward my

house. Sia knew something I didn't, especially to break the otherwise hours-long silence.

I didn't know what was going on, but I had to trust Sia. "Hey, let's take a detour, want to check on something." Left led to a rougher side of the city, some closed bars that the high school students regularly snuck into. Dani nodded, talking about something I couldn't focus on right then. A block passed, fewer people were around — how far into this place was Sia wanting me to go? I wasn't comfortable seeing homeless people on the side of the street, nowhere else to go. Or the buildings around, shattered windows, sewer-like smells hitting me like a brick wall.

"Kylie, we should turn around," Dani said, gripping my wrist. "You gotta be super tired, nothing's down here."

*"Don't. You're being trailed, and they're sloppy about it. Want to be noticed."* Sia prevented whoever was following from knowing where I lived. Had noticed something I hadn't the vaguest awareness of — even still, I couldn't identify *who* or *where* someone was stalking me. But Sia hadn't made up any prior emergencies, had given me no reason to think she was lying.

I locked my wrist, preventing Dani from jerking me away like a toddler on a leash. "Not yet." What could I say? What *should* I say? I knew nothing about the actual situation and even less on how to subtly convey something was wrong. "Though more guidance would *really* be appreciated," I said under my breath.

*"Straight, off to the right — I'm getting no auras from that... we'll say old gas station, I guess. Whatever you want to call it. Lead them into there, just stay steady."*

Auras? I had no clue what Sia meant but had to keep moving. "Let's check this area out," I said, my tone painfully fake with happiness. It hurt my ears; I had never considered myself a particularly bad or good liar, but right then was like a bad actress on a huge stage for how comfortable I was. Dani's confusion was like a siren blaring straight into my ears, and I didn't know how she hadn't caught on, but she made it even harder to stay *calm* like Sia wanted. I yanked my wrist free, running to the building Sia had pointed out.

"Kylie?" Dani ran after me.

Feeling dirt on my fingertips as I gripped the unlocked doorknob, the door creaked open, only light coming in from the grime covered windows — this place had been abandoned for years it looked, smelled like a skunk had exploded with one of the pine trees. "Okay...?" I asked, glancing around as I moved toward the light coming through the busted window, hoping to gain a better understanding of the building's layout. "Now what?"

"Seriously, Kylie — what the hell's so special in this dump?" Dani walked closer, moving her hands up to her chest as if the floor grime would crawl through the air and get on her. "Westside's just a slum, nothing here."

The door hinge creaked a bit more — from what? There was no wind. Dani was beside me...

Turning around, I saw a middle-aged woman, dark green eyes illuminated from the dimness of the building. Sia had been right, and I had been right to trust Sia. Hopefully Sia had a plan because there was something dangerous about this woman that I felt, a hunger and *admiration* from her, that made me step back.

*"My turn,"* Sia said. Instantly, I no longer had control of my body, a sensation I had only experienced after consenting to the loss of control every time before this. Sia asked no permission; I thought she needed consent to control my body but had just starkly discovered otherwise.

This was an emergency, though. It wasn't something Sia would do for no reason, right? Even though I tried to justify the circumstances, I hated my input was optional, felt like a violation I didn't know was even possible. It was one thing for there to be voices that ignored me, was another for them to take control of my body whenever they wanted.

"What do you want?" Sia said, using my body. Her eyes locked onto the woman.

"Kylie? You know who that is?"

The lips of the woman pulled into a slight smile. "It really is you."

I felt Sia's left hand make subtle moves, a slight sigh from her chest. "Don't make me repeat myself: state what you want."

That hunger increased even more. "To take you where you belong, back home."

"W-what's...?" Dani stepped back, bumping into something on the gray broken concrete that I couldn't make out because

Sia's eyes never left the woman, not even a momentary flinch from Dani's words or movement.

Dani's mood had shifted from annoyed to scared.

Scared? How bad was this for Dani to be scared? Dani was the one who scared off bullies when we had pre-k together. Well. Actually, in hindsight, Dani kind of *was* the bully then, but still.

"Surprise to us both, but not interested. Don't suppose we can just all walk out and go our separate ways?" Sia said. She glanced around to the left and right without moving her head — I wasn't sure what she was looking at. Was amazing how we saw literally the same thing, but I couldn't piece together what Sia was thinking or doing.

The lady shook her head. "You don't understand. It's for your own good."

"Well, you know what they say, some mistakes you just have to experience yourself. Pushing me on this will be yours if you don't leave right now."

Dani put her arm in front of Sia; she must not have figured out *I* wasn't the one talking. I wasn't exactly sure *how* she hadn't figured it out given how confident and almost bored Sia sounded, but also, most people didn't have others taking control of their body. I couldn't blame Dani for something she had never seen. "Don't worry, I'll protect you."

"Just... stay right there. Please." Sia said *please*? That word was in her vocabulary? I was learning all sorts of new things during this little misadventure. Sia dropped my backpack to the mildewed carpet I had been standing on; it intermixed from where it hadn't yet ripped to the concrete layer. The woman went missing. I felt something bang against my lower arm; Sia had raised her arm into a blocking stance faster than I could digest the moment. I felt the top of my sneaker bang into the woman's jaw before Sia back flipped into a kick and landed behind the woman. "This is my last warning: leave."

Some type of spike narrowly missed Sia, lodging in the building's rotting wooden frame structure. "You just *don't understand.*"

"Isare, heed your mistress's call, summon forth!" I felt metal in Sia's hands, something like a pole. It blocked another flail, this time lodging a spike into the concrete by Sia's feet.

How was Sia leaping and swinging and almost dancing through the air with my body? I hadn't taken ballet in years, since I could ditch it in middle school for extra honors work when I escaped from extra-curricular activities. Didn't know my body *could* move like this.

"I *said* I'll protect you!" Dani said as she charged the woman. Her strikes were fast, but they weren't steady like Sia's — a total lack of confidence; I felt terror in Dani's emotions, petrified yet *possessive*.

Circles emerged just above the concrete, like how they had *that day* for me. But this time, they weren't around me: they circled the woman, a yard long pointed ice projectile manifesting from her pointer finger.

Sia rushed forward at a speed that disoriented me despite still being my own body. "Just. Stay. Put." Sia's words were harsh, not the exhausted of before, not asking Dani but *ordering* her. "I don't have the resources right now to babysit you more than strictly necessary." The giant ice projectile sped through the air; Sia remained still; a strong wind rushed through the window, knocking the projectile off course into a concrete pillar and causing it to shatter into ice shards.

"Air manipulation... you really are her."

What? Who? What did that sudden breeze have to do with anything?

*"All mages have elemental alignment."* Kisate was actually providing helpful context for once. Truly was a day of surprises. *"Of course, with the purity of the royal line, I align with two elements: air and water."*

"Just be very, very thankful I'm working with the bare minimum." Sia used her left pointer finger to swipe up on the pole. Blades slid out from both sides. "But we're done here." She rushed forward at that same speed I didn't know my body was even capable of, closing the distance between herself and this strange woman in an almost instant. The blades sliced into the woman like a knife into steak, red dripping down the bladed edge of the pole, onto the woman, into the concrete and carpet. "Oh, you're actually alive. Yeah, that was really the wrong call on your part." A twirl of the pole, red coating the other end, like decorations of a dance. Screams of pain, feeling each slice as if it was on my body.

The woman fell back, her chest no longer moving, coated in blood. The pole disappeared from Sia's hands as she bent down to pick up the backpack. No blood was on it. On Dani. On myself, from what I could see. Everything had been calculated, precise. Sia was never out of control.

Had killed a woman with no hesitation at all.

"Wh-what happened to you?" Dani stepped further back.

I saw terror in her eyes, terror I couldn't blame, terror I felt. "This is why she hasn't been able to *hang out* with you. I'm not the Kylie you know. I'm one of those *voices* she's mentioned, the one she calls 'Sia.'"

"Give Kylie back."

"I'm not sure she wants control back at the moment, especially not until we're somewhere a bit more... familiar."

Dani rushed forward, gripping Sia's shoulders. I mentally winced and didn't know how Sia didn't physically do so because of the strength of Dani's fingers against skin. "Give *her* back, back to before all this, before *you people* took her away from me."

Sia moved her eyes away from Dani to the dead woman; I saw blood smeared and spreading further onto the concrete. I wish I could've puked but lacked a body to do so. The iron smell invaded my mind, and there was no way to block it out. "There is no 'back.' You all would've died if we didn't 'take' her. Is that what you want? For you both to have died instead?"

Dani's nails dug into Sia, the light tank top I wore doing little to shield my body from Dani's manicured nails. "Then take over me instead. I *have* to protect her."

"You can't. It's not a matter of 'taking over' a random teenage girl. This is something she was born with, something you were lucky enough *not* to be born with."

"Then that's it? You have all that power and shit and can't do a damn thing to fix this? Give me what ever happened to her, do it to me."

Sia's fist balled. "I can trigger Act for you. It's what causes active mana generation. But make no mistake, her current — let alone max — exceeds what you'll ever be able to reach. You can't be her. And the process won't be pleasant."

"I don't care. I'm not useless. I need to protect her."

"Fine." I hated how monotone my voice sounded from Sia right then as she slid my backpack on. Sia trained her eyes on Dani as the aquamarine and clouded blue-gray symbols with light in them appeared once more, this time under Sia. "Riyati, initiate transfer protocol, sustained supply." More characters on the lights — a few I even recognized from my Riyatian language studies — circled Sia.

Dani screamed. My heart and blood would've frozen at the sound if I had my body; even on *that day*, Dani didn't scream like this. She had passed out early in, especially compared to Jordan. Her chest heaved. "Act" was what I had the day all this started, when I'd first heard Sia in the forest... but it was nothing like this — why was Dani in so much pain? I felt it through my empathy, her body on fire, aching, like breaths ripped out of her chest.

*"She isn't compatible, and normally wouldn't have ever experienced Act; forcing it isn't pleasant. That's why I tried to warn her. But this is what she wanted, or at least says it is."*

I couldn't run or hide: my body was the one that had killed someone. Was torturing my oldest childhood friend regardless of Sia's claims that Dani "wanted" this. It wasn't; how would Dani have known? She just wanted to help, as she always had.

Sia couldn't be me. And I wanted nothing further to do with Sia.

# Chapter Eleven

## so much red

Jordan | May 8
North Opal Pines High

Dammit. It's faint, but I heard Mr. Smith's voice through the door while still in the hallway. I knew it's gonna happen, but there's still a new sense of foreboding doom from the stares and judgment that'd come as soon as I opened the damn door. I knew I was a fuckup that couldn't show up on time. No need to shove it down my throat more than it already was. Swallowing, I opened the door, a creak giving me away as they always did.

Mr. Smith didn't even turn around as he said, "That'll be detention tomorrow, Mr. Boyle."

"Yessir." I lowered my head as I tried rushing to my desk. Still hated all the attention on me right then. And yet again, Kylie's the only one that didn't look up, the only one I didn't mind receiving attention from gazing at something on her desk. Must've already been working on something. As I sat down, I noticed her planner out, but there's no writing. She'd placed her pen beside the rings on the planner, where it didn't look like it'd been touched since she sat down. Her eyes're puffy, something I couldn't remember seeing from her in years.

"Everything okay?" It obviously wasn't, but what other way was there to ask?

She shook her head.

The announcements kept going on and on as they always did, this time reminding the students that some type of parent-teacher event was coming up next week. Well, time for me to clock out 'cause wasn't like I had a parent that gave a damn.

"Your mom?" I asked. The most I'd ever seen her cry was back when we'd done a project together in early middle school. Was the last time I did a project with her — we got a C, and she'd been lectured and told how she'd fail out of everything ever. Ms. Rae'd lectured me too, but ain't like I had any expectations of being more than a drain on society to begin with. I hated seeing Kylie caught up in my bullshit though, didn't want her getting hell 'cause of me. Was a lot easier now with us not really sharing classes at all; there ain't much I could fuck up for her if I wasn't around. She'd not feel guilty 'bout being with another partner either, something else that'd happened when we were younger.

Another shake of her head. "I... I don't know how to even..." She rubbed her nose with the back of her hand; there were a few glances toward our conversation, but most of the class ignored us thankfully. "It wasn't a lie." She brought her hands together, one holding the other while being pressed into the laminate desk. "Someone tried... like *she* had said, like that day..."

"'She'?" There're so many "she's" with Kylie lately, I wasn't sure how she expected me to keep up. Then again, I had no idea what she was talking about at all. It obviously'd affected her, and I wondered why she's even in class right then. Why wouldn't she tell her mom something happened if Ms. Rae ain't the reason?

Unless it's something her mom couldn't know 'bout, didn't know 'bout. Like something that'd happened almost two months prior, back in March when the weather's pleasant instead of the humid hellscape of May.

"*That person.* She..." Kylie's voice dropped lower, almost a beg. "Isn't me. Can't be."

Siani. Something happened with Siani, and given I'd seen Kylie go off on people before, I could see Siani being just as much of a bitch. "Something with...the other stuff?" Magic. I wasn't sure why it felt forbidden to say it, but it did, 'specially right then.

A nod. "When Dani and I were walking home Friday..." The top hand's knuckles turned white from how hard she pressed into her other hand. "Someone tried to... to take me somewhere. I don't know where. But *she*... she..." Kylie swallowed before shaking her head. "Used *my* body to... and hurt Dani... the screams." The fact that there's no snide remark to one of those voices while Kylie spoke meant either she ignored them or that they're all silent.

The hell happened? Dani'd always treated me about like everyone else in this city: beneath her. Wasn't wrong, so I didn't really fault her for that. But she's taller than I am, wasn't the most approachable to begin with. Who'd be dumb enough to try something with her around in the first place?

"Someone tried to hurt you?"

She nodded. "Was stalking me for some reason. But... that was no excuse... there was..." Her voice dropped even lower; I strained my ears to hear her, 'specially over the other chatter in the classroom since announcements'd finished. "So much red."

A knot formed in my throat — red, blood. "From you?" She'd been hurt, had —

She shook her head.

If Kylie hadn't been hurt, and Sia'd been involved... that meant Siani'd killed someone, like that day that started everything, didn't it? Had protected Kylie and even Dani, it sounded. "But she had to, didn't she? Or else..." If it's like that day, then it's kill or be killed. There was no choice.

"She could've tried to call someone, or..." Kylie huffed. "I *told* you: I don't want to hear it." Ah, there's the now-frequent whole other conversation I'd never hear. A moment passed b'fore she snapped a bit too loudly, "Then explain Dani."

People glanced over at us, whispering something I couldn't hear while their eyes shifted between me and Kylie. "What happened?" I asked, hoping to redirect her attention away from the mental conversation and remind her we're in public and people're staring and I could do without even more damn rumors 'bout how she only talked to me out of pity and I'd fucked up. I didn't mind covering for her other conversations, but I absolutely wanted no more attention on myself.

Her head shot up for a second, like she'd forgotten where she was. "Sorry," she said. "I don't know. Dani wanted to be... like me." A pause came b'fore she added, "'Special.' And *she* basically tortured her, said it's because it was 'forced' or something, that Dani wasn't 'compatible.' The screams from Dani though. She doesn't have voices and didn't feel bad past the first night, but I kept checking on her because... I just... keep hearing those screams."

A week ago today I'd talked with Siani, hadn't known it was her, had looked just like Kylie, sitting in the seat she always does, where she sat right then. Siani's voice had been soft, knowing, like she saw through me, like she knew everything Kylie'd never pieced together. She'd scared the shit outta me, but she hadn't told Kylie. I didn't know why Siani hid it, why Siani knew where my bruises had come from, but just promised silence and had kept it as far as I could tell. She took away the damn throbbing that wouldn't stop, just like that day back in March when all this started. The Siani that Kylie didn't even acknowledge right then didn't match the one I'd briefly met both times. I didn't know why, but something didn't make sense.

I didn't dare say that to Kylie, however. Definitely not right then, likely never considering she wouldn't even say Siani's name; she'd rip my head off if I disagreed. "I..." What to say, though? I was sorry? But I had nothing to do with any of this. "I'm sorry." It's the only thing I knew. "It's been a sec since we went to the park." Maybe that wasn't the right thing to say considering the last time we went's when hell broke loose. She didn't budge, though, so I kept going. "Wanna go after school tomorrow? Well, after detention, I guess."

She couldn't reach out to Dani, not after what happened during the weekend. This's something even someone like me could assist with, could listen, 'specially when not in the middle of a classroom where we'd get stares and attention neither of us wanted.

She nodded, saying, "I'd like that." Kylie then softly winced, thankfully not loud enough to attract attention from any of the nearby classmates. "So much noise..."

The classroom ain't any louder than normal. "Huh?"

Her lips pressed together. "It's hard to explain. Just one of those... special things."

# Chapter Twelve

# perfect weapon

"How can you just sit there?" Kisate said. For not the first time recently, I half-regretted assisting Jordan with healing magic that day: Kisate had been going off on me near non-stop since then. For a mild blessing, she waited until my younger self was asleep, so I had kept my promise to Jordan, but still. It was getting old. Fast.

It was likely past eleven pm: Kylie was asleep, as was Chloé; typically, Kisate would've been in her own subcon where she wasn't my problem. It should've been a nice, contemplative time. A moment to hide away while the world was dark and all I had to do was maintain vague control over Kylie's empathy and fully block her sensory precognition. It was less strenuous compared to the daytime hours since she wasn't moving, experiencing things herself, and had no auras she was instinctively reading. "It's called respect. Look it up. Adeodowo."

"Do you not get it — he was hurt. How do you know it wasn't the same today? How do you know — "

"Because, in case you've forgotten, I'm the empath. Not you." Would've been a rather fascinating line of research to

**65**

examine why incarnations didn't maintain the same unique abilities across each incarnation. By all normal theory, Kisate's ability — whatever it was, I had no idea or interest in finding out — should've mirrored mine. It wasn't though, and that was especially apparent right then when I really was not in the mood to deal with this argument again. Not that Kisate would know, but Jordan's tells for when he'd been abused were rather consistent across both his emotions and pain levels; neither had been indicative something had happened since the last time Kylie saw him.

"Yet you don't intervene."

Other things I really regretted at the moment: subconscious principalities having even simulated physical presences. With Kylie asleep yet in control of her body, it meant that I was in the blackness of the subconscious principality, Leah off in an effective corner keeping an eye on my and Kisate's "conversation" but otherwise not getting involved. I sat with my head leaned back. My left hand was on my raised left knee, my right hand helping to support myself while right leg rested flat. Kisate marched up to me as if she wasn't emotionally and audibly loud enough as it was. No one respected empathic sensitivities.

If she wanted an answer that badly, she'd get one, but she wasn't going to like it. "Nope."

He owed me for this. He *so* owed me for this, in fact.

"He might die."

"Mmhm." Whether Kisate didn't notice or just didn't care, who knew, but I truly was not in the mood to entertain this fight for what felt like the thousandth time in like a week. As everyone that witnessed our interactions could attest, I wasn't one to back down from Kisate or a fight in general. But I didn't want to deal with it right then because other things were on my mind, and Kisate was getting in the way of trying to plan and process them. In short, she was in the way, and I was busy.

It was rather obvious she didn't like my answer, and even more obvious once she grabbed my hair and yanked me upward, like a doll on a string. "I am speaking to you. Know your place."

Slapping Kisate's hand away, I fully stood. Fine. She wanted my attention. She got it because that damn hurt. My aquamarine eyes met Kisate's light blueish-green ones. "I do. And it'd be wonderful if you did the same." That there were differences at all pissed me off more than usual.

"You only exist because of me."

I balled my left fist. It ached to connect with Kisate's face. How much had I cried over the years since I had Act? How much had I begged for peace, only to realize it never would never happen? How many times had I hurt myself? How many times had I watched chests stop moving?

How much had it hurt when I realized I wasn't even normal by mage standards, having been tampered with at a core, below-conscious level?

Yet another choice removed. And the origin of it all stood in front of me.

"You're right." I squeezed my fist tight enough that it would've bled from my nails had I had an actual body right then. "You made rather sure of that, didn't you?"

"I will be from this moment on: you answer to me."

I hardened my eyes. Rage wasn't an appropriate descriptor. It was deeper, more visceral. Blinding, wailing, begging. "I'm your ultimate weapon. Don't think I don't know about the blood magic you and Takite snuck in to alter myself and *the prince* instead of preserving mana to save Chloé and Dmitri. So get off your self-righteous throne and let the professionals work, preferably in peace."

"Don't say his name! You don't deserve it after what you've done, what you've allowed to transgress." She acted like I enjoyed letting things be. That it was fine seeing him in pain, that respecting Jordan's agency wasn't frustrating and difficult, like I didn't wonder if it was the wrong thing to do. But I wouldn't take a choice from him, and if all I could do was heal injuries right now, then that's what I would do. Moreso...

Who the hell was she to order me around like some pawn? I licked my lower lip as a smirk pulled to my lips. "Then make me. Should be nothing right? Just out-power me. Someone around for this long surely has willpower to spare, to speak nothing of cunning and theory knowledge."

I slipped, letting the empathic suppression on Kylie lapse for a moment, though I wasn't even sure exactly where I had done so. Controlling my own empathic abilities was one thing, but doing it twice at two separate ratios was entirely another and far more of a headache than I anticipated. Either way, she was awake now, in control of her body and outside of the subcon.

"Ow..." Kylie said. "Can you people like... not? What time is it even?"

"I'm demonstrating something, and you should take note as well. Maybe it will prevent this nonsense, assuming 'Siani' is truly who she claims to be."

Kisate kicked Kylie out of her body, flexing her hand; it must've been a literal flex of stealing control from Kylie, as if that was some type of impressive accomplishment. Rolling my eyes, I prepared for a logistics nightmare: managing multiple conscious shifts in succession. I focused, feeling Kisate having put up blocks around losing control of Kylie's body.

Cute.

"What's even going on?" Kylie asked, glancing around. She was barely half awake, though that was changing by the second as she groggily glanced around the subconscious principality, searching for answers that amounted to Kisate being a pretentious bitch.

I had already found a hole in Kisate's supposed iron-control, but I needed a way to lock Kylie in immediately afterward. Easiest way was probably to just knock Kisate out, which unfortunately would knock me out with her. Would be worth it though to knock that damn attitude down some though.

"Kisate thinks she's smarter than she is," I said. "You'll get control back in about fifteen seconds, though I'll probably be out a bit because of it. Either thank or complain to Kisate, your choice."

# Chapter Thirteen

# the same

I still wasn't exactly sure *what* that whole incident had been about the night before, but it had made today near hellish. This must have been the only time Sia was unconscious because my empathy was louder than ever before. Most of the day, I had struggled with not puking from the pain, but at least with school over, there were fewer people — emotions — to pick up on. I regretted not backing out of waiting for Jordan to finish detention. It had been a stubborn refusal for magic ruin more of my social life when he asked if we should cancel this morning, too tired to even process post-school during lunch, and now I wasn't even sure how I was walking home let alone maintaining a conversation or going to the park.

I hadn't forgiven Sia. I didn't trust Sia. But unfortunately, I had to admit that Sia most definitely had been doing *something* all this time, if for nothing else, keeping most of these empathic reads off my plate. And Sia needed to wake up sooner than later for there to be any shot of me going to school tomorrow because I was feigning sick if she wasn't awake before I went to bed tonight.

Resting my head on my desk, I felt the cool glossy laminate

wood against my feverish forehead. Apprehension. Didn't know where it came from or why or who was even on this side of the school at this point. Was the detention classroom nearby? I didn't know, hadn't ever been to it. Didn't really know much about it at all, I realized, only that Jordan was a frequent guest, and he grumbled a lot about it after being late too many times or cursing too much in a teacher's earshot. The first time I'd heard many of the curses in the English language had come from him, thinking about it: Mom found cursing to be *vulgar, uneducated.* That probably hadn't helped Mom's perception of Jordan, actually.

Another spike of emotion interrupted my thoughts. People just needed to stop feeling things. And Sia needed to wake up — whatever she and Kisate were squabbling about, never again. It was already disorienting that their arguing woke me up, spikes of intense emotions I hadn't been awake enough to identify. Then Kisate took over my body — which again, not something that I enjoyed knowing another could do, but that ship had sailed around the world multiple times for all my opinion mattered. Just as quickly, Sia somehow removed Kisate from control and put me back in, but it knocked them both out for whatever reason. Only Chloé and Leah were awake with me in the classroom, with Leah not sleeping all night and that weighing on her, as I had the pleasure of feeling on top of my own exhaustion and what felt like everyone in the hall's various emotions.

*"Kylie..."* Chloé said. *"You really should've just stayed home."*

If I stayed home every time magic had made me want to hide in my bed during the two months that had passed, I'd have missed more days than the rest of the year combined. Makeup work wasn't fun, and Mom couldn't know about this. I might have liked nothing going on, but Mom would flip and absolutely nothing positive could come of it. I was there, and I prayed Sia woke up any second. Also, it was too late to turn around, given the entire day was basically over anyways.

*"Sorry. Typically, Kisate handled this 'fore Sia, so never got good at it,"* Leah said. She hid the colored lights — auras — from my view. Another magic thing Sia had been controlling I didn't know existed prior to today. But Leah didn't know how to restrain empathy, only the auras, and even that was extremely

**70**

taxing on her. Chloé had tried to wake both Sia and Kisate up, but both were completely unconscious, something I could unfortunately confirm by one fewer emotion "signal" from within me: I couldn't identify most emotions beyond it feeling like someone screaming in my ear, but I developed some measure for proximity — except here in school, at least, where emotions were so much more complicated, likely because of the sheer density of people.

Annoyance. That same loudness, like a whisper in my ear, far away yet right there. Steady, not growing louder or quieter. It caused me to miss the classroom door opening. A man's heavy footstep shook me from my thoughts — was the annoyance from him? I'd never seen him before, but he was probably in his late twenties, decently dressed. Looked less exhausted than the average teacher in my high school. There was no increase in emotion as he stepped closer; the annoyance wasn't from him, begging the question of who it *was* from?

"It's time for you to leave," he said as he walked over to the window, closing the blinds. He must have been the teacher for this room, shutting it down for the day. I didn't know, had just found a random empty classroom still open so I could wait for Jordan. I would've waited in near the school entrance like normal, but I just wanted silence and rest while I could get it... not that said rest had actually happened given the density of emotions still crowding my brain.

"Oh, I'm sorry. I'll start packing up right now." Originally, I was supposed to do homework, but that hadn't happened — the moments of brief peace I had when emotions tapered allowed me to realize how exhausted I was from staying up half the night feeling Leah and Mom's emotions more intensely than before, and that had nowhere near prepared me for the onslaught of today's empath experience of a public high school. I didn't remember a word from any lectures given today, and I wasn't sure the few notes I took would teach me a thing later.

Moving my textbook to my backpack, I saw the man walk toward me. "Right, let's go." He grabbed my wrist.

"*Fuck. She was right,*" Leah said, which was *not* a tone I wanted to hear from her while Sia was still unconscious.

His grip increased as I tried to yank my wrist away, struggling with his strength compared to my own. "Let go," I said. Something was wrong. I didn't know if this was someone trying to kidnap me because of magic like this past weekend or something else entirely, but this man wasn't here just to shut down the classroom. I managed to push him forward while ripping my wrist back, separating us. The sudden movement caused me to fall backwards, slamming my rib into the metal desk leg. I winced, sharp inhale to my lungs from the pain.

The man had tripped back into the desks, causing a loud bang that echoed throughout the empty hallway. "He just wants to help you," the man said — I felt his aches pulse throughout my body, irritation and...

Concern?

A tap of shoes on the hallway — someone was coming, running even. Who was even here at this hour? What time was it even?

"Kylie, are you — " That was Jordan. "The hell's...?"

I wished I could give him an answer: I didn't know, and my head throbbed from *everything*. I had double vision. Sounds were loud and removed at once. What was a fatigue illusion and was the man really coming closer and closer to me again? I shook my head. "No..."

"She needs to go. Be where she belongs."

There was a whimper from Jordan as the man gripped my wrist, yanking me from where I hadn't been able to pull myself up after slamming into the desks. His hand was rough, cold, friction stinging against my skin from how tight his grip was.

*"Wait. Fuckin' hell, did she plan this?"* Leah asked. I didn't know who Leah referred to or the answer to that question because I lacked context and, more importantly, had absolutely no energy to even ask for clarification. Those *auras* briefly covered my vision — dark green from the man and this vivid deep dark red and dark blue from Jordan's direction. It disappeared as quickly as it had come, Leah recovering control.

"Let's not." That was Jordan's voice. But that wasn't a tone I had ever heard from Jordan: secure, calm. Serene.

There was a clash, a thud. The man's grip over me disappeared, Jordan catching me as I fell back. Everything hurt.

"G...get away..." There was no Sia to save us, not like she had done with Dani. Whoever this was just wanted me, not us both.

"You're the same — you should understand," the man said. I strained to make words out, everything removed and too close and ringing. Emotions overwhelmed every inch of me, none of them my own. Annoyance shifted to terror, matched only by an even more confusing... something. Something soft, positive. I didn't have a word for it, especially not right then. I gave up trying to figure out who felt what; nothing made sense, and I wanted to just sleep, to stop the onslaught that had been this nightmare.

Calloused fingers rested on my bare arms and supported me as I tried to stand. "Touch her again and you're not walking away. Welcome to go crying like a whipped bitch to your master though. Only way you're making it outta here, actually. Your choice."

"He knows best — you're just a child."

A sigh, a sensation of irritation pulsing through my mind. "Fine, your death, not mine."

And that was when my consciousness gave out.

# Chapter Fourteen

## string to the neck

Glancing to the chair beside my own, I saw it was empty despite homeroom only having a few minutes left. Jordan was habitually late but almost never absent, and this was far past his normal late time of rushing in. I bit my lip — was he all right?

*"Probably passed out. You were out most of the morning the day after your Act, and I offloaded some of the strain. It doesn't sound like that happened for him."*

For him.

When I had woken up, I wasn't kidnapped or even in a classroom: I was in my bed, shoes and backpack placed next to my desk, tucked in under my covers and no one else around. Sia had woken up by then, no more emotion-sirens running through my head. I tried asking Leah and Chloé what happened in case they took control after I blacked out, but they both stammered. No firm answer.

Sia had a soft voice as she asked, "He had Act, didn't he?"

Act — "Activation" — was what happened to me in March. What happened to Dani not even a week prior.

What happened to Jordan yesterday.

Since Jordan wasn't present for me as a cover for

75

conversations with the various personalities inside me, I wrote "did you know" on a blank page of my notebook.

There was a rush of panic. Couldn't have been from Sia — I wasn't sure Sia knew the definition of "panic." At least one if not all three of the others, though...

*"Mm. I had to, you knowing now and all."* Her voice didn't have the usual confidence, instead being almost reflective, a soft tone to it similar to the question she'd asked Leah and Chloé the day before.

I wrote out "the others?" That panic rush returned: confirmation one if not all of them knew. Another scribble: "Why did no one say anything?"

*"Because she said not to,"* Kisate said, a tone of satisfaction present. "She" could've only meant Sia. *"I wanted to say something because he —"*

*"So you're saying you listen to me all of the sudden?"* Sia asked. That promptly stopped Kisate mid-sentence, leading to a silence.

The end information was the same though: Sia knew and somehow convinced the others to say nothing. If Kisate knew, then Leah and Chloé also most certainly did as well. Sia wanted the information withheld, and it was yet another indication that whatever her goal was, it wasn't in my interest and the interest of those around me. Just like how she killed that woman with my body; just like how she near tortured Dani with Act despite it not being at all painful for me.

I didn't know why Sia lessened the effects of the auras and empathy, why I got that one grace. I couldn't outright rebel against Sia because of it, though. Like a string to my neck that I didn't know had been there prior to the previous day, I had to comply because otherwise, I wouldn't be able to survive.

Squeezing the pencil tighter, I wrote, "do you know where he is? Is he okay?"

Sia chuckled, and I didn't like I had no read on why the question was humorous to the older girl. *"I wonder."* When I tried to press further, she wouldn't clarify, wouldn't say anything. I didn't know where he lived; he'd always been "around" but always avoided giving any actual addresses, and he'd never had a cellphone.

While I knew the concern I felt was my own for once, it

didn't really matter: I was just as helpless to soothe it as if the feelings belonged to someone else.

# Chapter Fifteen

## mistake

Jordan | May 10
Boyle Residence

Fuck, everything hurt. This was different than normal pain too — wasn't like something's injured, instead's like I'd had a damn PE final. Wasn't even taking the damn class this year. Everything's silent too; usually Thomas's banging around, getting ready for school. Or at least he better had been 'cause so help his ass if I was late *again* 'cause he couldn't be bothered to get dressed in time 'cause he got distracted with the damn dictionary again. How the hell's a *dictionary* entertaining to begin with? Sure, I was around the library a lot during summer, but that's 'cause it had AC, not 'cause I actually enjoyed being there.

Opening my eyes, I saw I was alone.

Actually, why was I home at all? Last I remembered, there's that creep trying to take Kylie somewhere, then a feeling, like something snapping inside me, a glass wall shattering that caused exhaustion and energy at once.

That's it, all I remembered.

I was still in my school clothes, but I was on my bed, light coming in through the blindless window.

Actually. Why's the sun out at all? I never slept this late, was usually up not long after Thomas. Definitely was no way I slept through the commotion of Jewel and Thomas getting ready for school. Right?

But that's what had happened, the only thing that made sense. The only reason I was alone, the only reason the sun shone in the window.

What'd happened to Kylie? That creep didn't —

*"Steady there. She's fine."* I heard a voice in my head: masculine, similar to my own but older by at least a few years. *"Rotanu took care of her."*

Rotanu?

Where'd that voice even come from? Didn't even sound like anyone's in the apartment for once, not even father snoring after blacking out. Pure silence.

"Hello?" I said, glancing toward the door out to the living room. Still no one.

*"Denial's a bitch,"* another masculine voice said. Where...?

*"I would've thought you'd be a bit, uhm, more patient considering things, Rotanu."*

Voices no one else could hear, a story I'd heard rather frequently lately from one aquamarine eyed girl.

But I was no one. Nothing.

This was wrong.

I had to get to school, check on Kylie. Maybe I accidentally drank something and was hallucinating. Something to give reason to these voices and —

Sitting up, I winced, holding my head. Everything burned, muscles bitching loud complaints.

*"It's been like eighteen hours. Why's it so bad still?"* Another voice. This one's younger than the other two, startling close to my voice.

*"I had to push a bit to get things wrapped up yesterday. Will be fine."* That's the voice named Rotanu. As if remembering I heard their conversation, Rotanu said, *"Initial cycle's a bitch. You'll be feeling it for a few days, but it'll taper. Nothing wrong, just how it goes."*

Bullshit. It's all wrong.

I winced as I pulled myself from bed, rushing as much as I could to the front door to put my tennis shoes on; I grabbed my keys and stepped outside, locking the apartment behind me.

*"Will you calm your ass down? You're making it hell on me now, which's just gonna bite your ass when I slip."*

"'Slip'?" I whispered so no one around would hear me.

*"Someone's handling the disconnect between your bitch-fit and you frying this whole damn city. That's me, by the way."*

Rotanu's apparently the chatty one *and* the one handling — no. This wasn't real. Was a dream. Was a hallucination and I was still in detention and —

Colors were everywhere, outlines where people stood: the more crowded, the denser, more colorful and overwhelming the outlines became. The fuck's this? The lights weren't consistent at all — most were faint, but different colors, and so many, and just... everywhere.

*"Dammit,"* Rotanu hissed.

My eyes widened as smoke emerged from the grass I'd walked on. I saw the entrance to the park and dashed in — whatever the fuck's going on, at least in the forest I'd be alone. If a mass murderer could get away for months, I'd be fine while working out whatever mistake this was. Muscles further strained, my lungs aching as I tried to force oxygen down them. Thankfully, the park's almost completely abandoned; there was only one color — a faint green — from some blonde haired guy reading a book on one bench toward the entrance. I ran past him, into the forest section, as the grass still singed beneath my shoes. Trees covered in front and behind me; I kept running, tightening my eyes, until I collapsed to my knees.

I hadn't even questioned whether this's something I should hide: I knew. Don't be seen. Don't let everyone know I was an even bigger freak than I had known.

I hiccupped, air not coming to my lungs fast enough. Destroyed trees were all around me: bark to ashes, plants frozen despite it being May and easily in the 80's. A bead of sweat dripped down my forehead. I had done this.

It was all a mistake.

# Chapter Sixteen

# good morning kiss

Siani | May 13
Training House

It had taken an impressive amount of restraint to not rip control from Kylie and never give it back. More restraint than she would ever know. ...Well, until she was "Siani" at least. That had been the longest two months of my life, which was quite an accomplishment considering my "shouldn't be here right now" resume.

"Are you sure this is the right place?" Kylie asked, her eyes darting around. We were on the West Side, perfect for what I had planned. Jordan was beside her, uncomfortably shifting his weight to his right side. Probably too close to home, so to speak, maybe even literally right then. I hadn't kept up with all the places "Rota" had lived over the years, but I knew the general areas weren't as far from here as Jordan would've liked given Kylie's oblivious discomfort.

*"You don't want to be somewhere recognizable, trust me. It being abandoned is actually to your benefit. We'll talk more about why later, but for now, just know you do not want to openly use magic outside of specific areas where no one's around. Bad things will happen if you do."*

Kylie pushed the jammed metal door, hearing a clank as it opened. This entire neighborhood had been effectively abandoned, casualty of textile work drying up a few decades back. It meant that there might've been a few people around, but they weren't people who knew Jordan or Kylie, and they weren't the type to ask questions to begin with, weren't the type to ever have polite or cooperative conversation with anyone resembling authority. Perfect for what we needed.

*"Can I take over?"* I asked.

Kylie bit back a huff as she nodded. We both knew I didn't actually need to *ask*, and it was a polite gesture more than anything else, something that Kylie was not amused with. Unfortunately, that wasn't exactly something that I could really fix, at least not yet. One day.

I took control of Kylie's body and opened my left palm, creating a light orb to act as a flashlight. Widening the diameter, I let it float up while I set up more sustainable lighting.

*"Why can't I learn more useful things like that?"* Kylie grumbled.

There was no reason to split my consciousness. "You will, but one step at a time. Also *just saying* I was *not* the one that went on a two-week tangent about the Riyatian character set being the absolute first step." I felt a spike of argument, but it wasn't from Kisate, who had been remarkably quiet for a blessing since she hadn't gotten a victory she thought was all but secured the night of her tantrum. Instead, this irritation was more *purposeful*. And there was only one person who knew how to weaponize my empathy against me: "Rota, don't even start on me."

Jordan said nothing and to his credit, Rota didn't take control when I half-wondered if he would; to be fair, he likely didn't because he knew I was reading emotions and would catch his reaction.

*"'Rota'?"* Chloé asked. I could hear it in her tone, she knew, uncharacteristically cautious yet hopeful. Leah was awake but said nothing; it hurt too much, could feel her longing and hesitance.

Jordan shifted his weight once more, still glancing around. No doubt, they exchanged words on his end as well. Words that we couldn't hear.

Ten people in a room with only two bodies a complicated communication hell.

"Mm. Like me," I said, my tone quieter. I raised my voice back to catch Jordan's attention. "Anyways. Rota needs a nice wake-up call, and I need to make sure of a few things that he's very generously going to assist me with." Opening the bag Kylie had brought, I took the battery-operated portable lamps out, turning them on; I tossed one Jordan's way, and the fact that he caught it without struggle indicated Rota had kicked Jordan out of control. "You can help, you know."

"Putting me to work not even a week in. Don't ever get a damn break." There was movement behind me, a soft clank of plastic touching the concrete flooring.

"You know what you signed up for, don't even start."

Turning around, I saw we had reasonably spaced the lamps, lighting up the abandoned flat. "This is your new training space for practical application: you don't want explosions in your bedroom, go figure."

"*Explosions*?" Kylie asked.

"Mm. They're fun." Actually, mines were one of my favorites, and they were technically not part of the explosion spell category; there was just something so incredibly satisfying about laying mines down and watching enemies stomp on them and get incinerated from waterized lasers. No one ever listened when I tried to share the joy, though, which was such a shame.

I glanced around, seeing the kitchen area — no appliances remained or had for a while. Place was barren — if it wasn't literally attached to the floor or ceiling or wall somehow, it had been long since stolen or sold or otherwise removed. That made it perfect though: was an old flat, full brick and concrete. Could take a beating. And it would.

My hand went to Kylie's absorption device.

"Kyle?"

I instinctively turned toward his direction before shaking my head; only *he* called me that. "Sorry, reminiscing. I'm pulling for alt form just to avoid dealing with clothes. Not a bad idea for you to verify I did the auth's right before having Jordan try later. Would rather find out now if I need to recheck something."

How I could simulate my physical form and magipoten for Kylie despite the technical difficulty of *not existing yet* was probably a complicated enough procedure that an entire book could be written on it. It didn't get less complicated altering the process to allow for Rota's form and magipoten to also be simulated for Jordan. Thankfully, I didn't need to explain my methods to anyone, and it was better that I didn't. The result was all that mattered: when using the "alt form," Jordan and Kylie would have access to Rota and my mana and magipoten's instead of their own — something that should've been impossible.

"Full I'm assuming?" Rota asked. He was probably the one closest to understanding how the technicalities for this spell functioned, but even then, he still couldn't have truly laid it out because he was too busy reading damn history books and complaining at me all the time about the little theory I managed to shove down his throat.

"Preferably, if his supply can take it."

Rota hesitated a moment, eyes lowering. "Tight, but should be fine. He'll just sleep like hell tonight." Even if the mana needed to go into alt form was negligible, it was still extensive considering Jordan just had Act about a week prior on top of having a lower estimated max magipoten than Kylie.

*"Wait, this is going to hurt Jordan? Why not me?"*

"Because you've had two months of magic build up. He's had like a week. Makes a difference."

Kylie said nothing in response, but she didn't lash out either. Some form of progress.

The words came so easily to my lips, words I had said so many times prior: "Riyati, obey your mistress's command, activate withdrawal." As expected, the simulation of my form — in my time, in my age — occupied the space where Kylie's body had been. For the first time since Kylie's Act, I felt my full mana supply be tethered. One day, Kylie would have to memorize the phrase, commit it to the deepest parts of her memory. But that day wasn't here yet, and I would take control until it was. And in the meantime, it felt good to be *myself*, even if for only a brief period.

*"This spike?"* Kisate said. *"How? This is — this is more than even Leah had."*

I wasn't enough of a bitch to answer that question: because I had lived post-Act longer than Leah had, I had a chance for my magipoten to continue increasing. Instead, I let the question hang in the air and nodded to Rota. "Go ahead, I'm monitoring for hiccups."

"Phrase established?"

I chuckled. "Figured you remembered it enough to remind me."

"Nope, forgot, sorry."

Rolling my eyes, I tilted my head. "Well?"

"The joke's — never mind, I'll explain later," he said. I doubted it was to Jordan, probably was to one of the other incarnations. Jordan's emotions were the equivalent of trying to hide under his bed and never come out, so the fact he was here at all was something.

I hoped Rota wasn't as rough on him as I suspected had already happened. Coming face to face with the past wasn't easy, and Rota had never been especially fond of his own.

"'Ice and fire, merge into one, release.'"

Nodding, I said, "Riyati, access stored blueprint relative, bind to aura for continued permission renewal until access revoked. Allow direct withdrawal and simulation of specified blueprint based off aura specifications." Two glyphs opened, one under me — my aura colors of teal and clouded blue-gray filling the spell's authorizations and parameters. The other appeared under Rota, his own aura filling the glyph under him — deep blue and scarlet red. "Phrase set: Ice and fire, merge into one, release."

The glyph beneath Rota and I both closed.

Rota stretched his neck to the left and then right, taking a deep breath before releasing it. The fun thing about experimental spells was there were always new and exciting ways for things to go wrong, which was something Rota had experienced firsthand way more than once during our practices. "Ice and fire, merge into one, release."

I monitored the simulation blueprint pull along with the simulation power withdrawal; everything seemed aligned, and Jordan's physical body shifted, replaced with the Jordan of my time: Rotanu. In combat gear sure, but I bit my lip, wanting to be home, where this was the norm, the always, instead of a passing moment.

It wasn't the time for nostalgia.

"Stable?" I asked.

He nodded. "What other shit you got planned? No way you're letting me off here."

A smile pulled at my lips. "Of course not. That'd be too easy for all the slacking you've had the past two months."

"Ain't a good morning kiss good enough catch up?" he grumbled. It wasn't quiet enough for Kylie to miss, me to miss, and certainly not for Jordan to miss. I glanced away, a slight blush on my cheeks. That was something he wasn't exactly supposed to mention, not yet. And I'd bet it wasn't even intentional on his end, just his routine sulking. He mumbled, "Shit," confirming my theory.

"So, about the wall?"

"No." He shot that down predictably quick.

Change of topic didn't save me. Leah wasn't surprised, Chloé wasn't surprised, Kisate *certainly* wasn't surprised because she made damn sure of it. Two people in the room *were* surprised, however: Kylie and Jordan. The latter would've been blushing and maybe stammering, but otherwise wouldn't have said anything. *Kylie,* however, had plenty of thoughts on this topic and I *felt* them oncoming.

*"You? With? No. That seals it. I don't know who you are, but I would never —"*

I didn't want this argument. Hated I still resonated with her in so many ways on this topic. But I couldn't deny the fundamental truth Rota had let slip: I wasn't just friends with him, wasn't even "just" his girlfriend. I was engaged to him, to the Jordan of the future.

# Chapter Seventeen

# break the ice

Rotanu | May 13
Subconscious Principality

Hadn't been back a week and Kyle'd already had my ass busy. Typical, and I wished I was more surprised than I was. As I'd expected, Jordan barely made it home 'cause of the fatigue from the alt form spell; he passed out around seven pm, early even for him. Us.

Fuck, this's disorienting.

I wasn't as fortunate: was mentally wide awake yet Jordan's body needed the rest, so wasn't like I could try to burn the energy off cleaning or anything I normally would've done if I wanted to tire myself out.

...Wasn't like there's a shortage of shit to clean in this rendition of my family's apartment, either; could've used all the love I could give it and then some. Typical, but was annoying as all fuckin' hell to see, regardless.

Prior to this week, it'd been over three years since I'd last been in a subcon, and now it's my new home for the next while. I'd intentionally skimmed as many books as I could find prior to leaving my time. Basically had created a multi-year digital library in my head, and now I had more than enough time to go through it, likely many times over. Taking a deep breath, I attempted to focus. Yet again in my life, magic's much more Kyle's thing than my own, and yet again, that sucked. Opening my eyes back, I focused on recreating one text to see if I could. Should've really tested this prior to now, but hindsight's ever a bitch.

"You said, you call yourself 'Rotanu'," Takite said. Or asked. I wasn't exactly sure which it was.

It's the first time any of my prior incarnations approached me. I hadn't been with them for years and years as was typical, just a random consciousness slid in sometime recent — either at Kyle's Act or my own, I wasn't sure which, though she probably knew more specifics than I'd ever care to hear.

Maybe me and Kyle talking helped break the ice. Or maybe it made more questions that they wanted answered. Was time to find out regardless of if I was ready or willing.

"It works, yeah."

"You're..." Takite opened his mouth, hesitating. He had on formal Riyatian attire, the same as he had died in. Didn't connect how that was morbid as fuck when I was younger, but damn. We were all around the general appearance of our last appearance, but he was the only one that was the exact same, down to his clothes; his shoulder length hair was around my length but better maintained, his nails neatly filed and an engagement ring on his marriage finger. Not sure how Riyati called that one so far in advance, but it was hilariously close, just a full ring instead of a band, ruby in the center.

I rubbed the back of my neck, glancing away. "Yeah, like 'Sia' is Kyle — Kylie — at 20, same for me; I'm Jordan, same age." Where's Kyle to go off on a magic tangent when I needed her? Wasn't fair I was stuck giving out damn explanations when I sucked at them.

"Does..." Another voice — John. Second incarnation, hair shorter than my own. Was a soldier, had met the notorious thief that's Leah on one of her heists, fell for her and eventually watched her die. At least he had on traveling clothes, not the exact same as he died in. It's a depressing bar to surpass, but that's apparently my new standard. "She really...? To 20?" There're a lot of technicalities that Kyle'd have such a blast with on that statement; I could already hear 'em despite her not even being there. It didn't matter: the answer John wanted and even needed was my nod. "Does he just not...? After what happened last time..."

No one wanted to say what happened last time. Not that it mattered, I knew: Chloé died. Incarnations're only bound to the next incarnation forward if there's an unclean death. All of Kyle's incarnations died unclean deaths.

All of my incarnations're the same.

Dmitri had wide eyes that would've fooled most, 'specially right then, watching me as if I had every answer in the world. He wasn't far off in appearance from the Jordan of this time, which made sense given they're similar in age. He's much more innocent appearing than the older and wearier John or withdrawn Takite. Chloé and him'd never really gone beyond puppy love, hadn't ever had the opportunity to. Dmitri only realized his feelings after she was gone. It's those eyes I was against, eyes that made me want to say everything when I didn't know what I could or couldn't or should or shouldn't say. I didn't know the line, wasn't some grand mastermind. This whole setup had Kyle's goddamn name all over it, not mine. But... even still... "Kyle'd have my ass if she knew I was saying even this, but..." Takite, John, and Dmitri all exchanged glances between one another. I didn't know if it was disbelief or hope or distrust. But I knew their pain better than they would prob'bly ever know. That's why I offered a reassuring smile. "That's why we're here, to make sure there's never another episode like what happened to Chloé, to Leah, ever again."

# Chapter Eighteen

## all wrong

"No, your form's all wrong," Dani said. She had crossed her arms, standing a few feet away within the personal gym her parents had changed their partially finished basement into. There were mirrors on all sides of the room, reflecting me back at myself no matter the way I turned; colorful foam pads were under my feet, hard yet squishy. A few punching bags hung from the ceiling while there was a rack in the back corner with weights and gloves and some other things I had never identified: while it was most definitely not my first time in the room, it was my first time being there for more than a handful of minutes, and it was the first time I was an active participant here instead of fetching Dani for her parents.

When I had said I wanted more of my life back away from magic, this was *not* what I meant. I meant normal things, like actually getting to study for my finals in like a week and a half or forbid, doing normal teenage girl things like actually spending time with my friends or scrolling through social media in my pj's all weekend.

Things I used to do. Things I was most definitely not indulging in right that second. Dani could go back to lecturing about how no boy was good enough for her, how she was mad at her mom's detective work at the station making dinner late or her father being overseas on a business trip again; any of those would've been an improvement to my current situation, where Dani attempted to teach me some basic martial art stances she knew. Problem being, *attempting* was a rather strong word for how *nit-picky* Dani was.

I hadn't even moved from the *last* time Dani fussed my foot was too far over or something. As before, Dani came close, hands pushing and yanking my limbs in various directions.

Even worse, I still had empathy, which of course increased with touch as usual: Dani's heart raced, something in the realm of awkward but not quite it flashing through her as she nit-picked over each inch and even sub-inch difference. It made my heart race as a biological response, and that irritated me even further: empathic reads I yet again did not want or need. Was there an empathic read that I ever wanted? The whole thing felt like a continuous dumpster fire to my emotional fortitude.

Taking in a deep breath, I released it, attempting and mostly failing to calm my body down. "I need a minute," I said.

"Oh sure." I wished I missed Dani's comment under her breath that we hadn't even been practicing long, how out of shape I was. At least Dani stepped away, letting me walk to my water bottle and drink some.

This had been a *bright idea* of Sia's: I get typical teenage sleepovers back. Yet again, I should've read the fine print on that idea because this was *not* what I meant by a sleepover, even if I had indeed slept over the previous night and even watched a movie with Dani. Dani absolutely jumped onto the idea and even encouraged Sia to just teach *both of us* in magic training. So, I had whatever martial art training thing I was failing miserably now, with Sia teaching me and Dani magic theory later in the day before I headed home. Somehow, my weekends had gotten *worse*, not better. Leah and Chloé were talking about something as well, and I wish they had gone into their own subcon-thing because that wasn't helping my rapidly vanishing sanity.

Coming back to where Dani was, I grumbled, "Why's Jordan get out of this? Shouldn't he be stuck in whatever this is too?"

The comment was completely meant for Sia: Kisate had been uncharacteristically quiet since that night before Jordan's Act.

"Why would *he* be here?"

I almost squeaked on hearing that I had not been quiet enough.

*"I'd answer that, but I think you're about to be a bit busy."*

"Um." Lying wasn't a likely choice: while Dani and Jordan didn't know each other well, they knew *of* each other very well; in fact, Dani had never been particularly fond of him, something that had always endeared her to Mom. "No reason."

I didn't want to come closer and feel Dani's... what was this? Anger? Not quite, there was almost sadness in it. Disappointment? In what, though?

Until empathy, I thought I had a good grasp of the human emotional spectrum. Unfortunately, I was extremely incorrect, and emotions were far more intangible, messy, and clouded than I had ever dreamed.

"And you were talking to *her*, weren't you?"

Dani was also not the greatest fan of Sia despite supposedly wanting training from her, and while I was usually first to jump on the Dislike-Sia ship, there were a handful of problems: first, no matter what else I felt or believed, Sia had been correct that attempts had been made on my life. That led to the second problem: if I wanted to live, I needed to be able to protect myself; the very existence of Sia implied that she wouldn't be there to protect me forever, and while I had no qualms about having just *myself* in my head, I was a sitting target at the moment. Third: I needed Sia, and if Sia was indeed telling the truth about her existence, Sia needed me.

In other words, I didn't have to *like* Sia, and I certainly hadn't forgiven her, especially not after that implication from the supposed future Jordan. Sia had killed someone, had tortured Dani, had decided to date what should've been a friend since childhood, a fight I had been trying to dispel for years to our classmates as it was. But I unfortunately had to recognize some amount of compliance with her was in my interest.

That said, I just nodded in response to Dani's question: I was talking to Sia and really wished I knew how to reply mentally, like Sia had done the few times she controlled my body. It would've been an incredibly useful skill for moments like these.

"And again, why would he be here? Why would *she* even care to begin with? Does she have a crush on him or something?"

That was entirely too close to the truth, and I wasn't thrilled to confirm it in any manner. Was something I preferred not to talk or even think about myself, actually. "I. Um." My hand moved to my absorption device, seeking its warmth. Dani's irritation increased further, causing me to step back in an attempt to lessen the empathy reads. I would've asked Sia to turn that down even further, but I didn't dare try to say a word to anyone but Dani right then with how quickly Dani's mood had soured from just one question.

It was like Dani wanted to pretend it was only us in the room when that was something I couldn't even pretend; Dani wasn't the one who had people after her; Dani didn't *have* to learn and do all this extra stuff just to survive.

I backed up against one of the punching bags, felt the cool fake leather softly bounce against my shoulder blades from where I had bumped into it.

"Well? Are you going to tell me or just leave me in the dark all day?"

Another deep breath. I focused on the cold leather against my skin.

I nodded, lowering my gaze to the lined patterns against the foam pads, to the different colors placed down — mostly blues with some yellow squares more recently added. "Last Tuesday, after school, there was this guy. He... he tried to kidnap me, like that woman did on that Friday when I was with you." I barely remembered the second kidnapping attempt and was fortunate Jordan had "Act" when he did: I would've been kidnapped had it not been for the "future Jordan," Rotanu. I might've even been dead.

It was terrifying. It was something I didn't even want to consider.

It was something I couldn't afford the luxury of ignoring.

Dani rushed forward, her hand on my arm, holding the skin tighter than I appreciated. Dani was just as terrified as me, immediately understood the severity. "Did she...?"

I shook my head. "Sia wasn't conscious, her and Kisate had

gotten into an argument the night before, and she was out from it. Rotanu did. He's like..." How to describe this connection that I didn't believe. Didn't want to be true. Couldn't be true. "He's to Jordan like Sia is to me. He's the one that saved me."

Dani's grip increased, fingers pressing into my arm bone. Not enough to hurt, but definitely enough to be uncomfortable. "What do you mean *saved you*? He's... he can't even hold a conversation, let alone fight off someone like that woman was. He's a wimp. Hell, half the time his clothes are patched up from what I've seen, doesn't even dress properly. There's *no way* he would protect you better than I would."

I had no words for Dani: I was offended at the remarks about Jordan. Sounded the same as all my classmates, the same arguments Mom had used for years and years. Maybe that's even where Dani got some of her arguments. But her emotions held a fear and even insecurity that I didn't understand. Rendered all arguments silent because everything I said seemed to hurt Dani, and that wasn't what I wanted, either.

I didn't know what to say or feel or do anymore. Everything was all wrong.

# *Chapter Nineteen*

## changes

Jordan | May 17
Boyle Residence

When I'd watched Kylie deal with Siani, I thought nothing'd really changed for her. She mentioned a foreign alphabet or just argued with voices I never heard.

I wasn't sure if it's just my shitty luck that I ended up with the useless "older self" or if Kylie's hell'va more graceful than I ever realized.

Maybe it's both.

I scrubbed burned debris off the stove, left there by someone that wasn't me 'cause I knew not to do shit like this. Prob'bly's Elaine, never bothered to pick up or clean a damn thing. Half the time, me or Jewel're stuck taking her laundry down to the wash 'cause she left her shit everywhere. Even though Elaine's the oldest, she acted as damn inept as Thomas.

The sponge's temp changed from room temperature to scalding, steam erupting from it, which led to a mild burn against my right pointer finger. "Fuck," I yelped. Double checking the stove's off, I huffed. "If you're gonna *literally* freeload in my head, can't you do your one damn job?"

It wasn't the first of these incidents since my *"Act"* just over a week prior. The worst had been the afternoon I seared and froze a section of the forest, where that blonde-haired guy almost found out I'd been the *cause* of that shit show. Only thing that saved my ass's I'd been just as confused as him, not knowing why the bark's frozen or grass's singed. I hadn't fully comprehended *I'd* done it, and now I wished I'd go back to that bliss. Further confirmation'd come from repeat instances, all at least milder. It'd become an almost daily occurrence: any emotional variance at all, something froze or burned. Sometimes it's "and" instead "or." And one've those repeat instances just fuckin' happened again: the sponge had charcoal where my pointer finger'd been.

*Rotanu* was supposed to be preventing shit like this, but he sucked ass at it.

"*Stop being so damn mopey. You act like it's easy remote controlling this shit.*"

"Seems to be easy enough for Siani. Haven't seen Kylie with something scalding her ass."

"*First off, no shit I'm not gonna compare to Kyle — this's her thing. Second, you just haven't noticed it for her since she doesn't have ice or fire aspect; her's wind and water, and notice how shit gets humid around her sometimes or there's a strong-ass breeze? Yeah. That ain't random, so leave my ass alone.*"

I was fortunate enough to be alone in the kitchen. This nonstop chatter'd been hell when people're around; I understood Kylie's desire to have someone else to *pretend* to talk so she could actually participate in conversations; I just couldn't whisper soft enough for people to not overhear me.

"*Not to interrupt... whatever you two are having,*" Takite said. Pretty sure he actually completely intended to interrupt. "*But I could work with Jordan on basic manipulation control if that'd help. I know Rotanu's handling most of the other sensory modifications, so that would lessen the burden there while keeping Jordan a bit more out of harm's way.*"

"*Be my guest,*" Rotanu said. The tone was different, though I couldn't pinpoint exactly how. It's like he'd been expecting it, not surprised at all.

"*Jordan?*"

"Fine, whatever." I wanted nothing to do with any of this. This's Kylie's thing. I just was meant to watch from the side, cheering her on. But... it'd be really nice to stop experiencing both frost and normal burns. Nothing'd been harmful enough yet, except... It should've been. Turning my hand over, I saw no burn mark at all on my pointer finger or anywhere else from the other incidents. "The hell...?" Most of the burns'd been on my dominant hand, but I checked my left as well to be sure. Nothing.

*"Is something wrong?"* Takite asked.

It felt strange to ask why I ain't hurt; was similar to the disorienting moments where Siani'd healed injuries. But she's nowhere around this apartment. My hand should've been full of burns with how this past week'd been. "Why wasn't — " I didn't even know how to ask. "There should be burns."

*"Doesn't work like that anymore,"* Rotanu said. *"Part of the changes going on with an increased amount of mana in your system."*

There's a lot to unpack from his words, and I liked none of it. "The hell you mean?"

Dmitri's typically the quietest one, almost meek. He's the closest to me, both in age and demeanor. That made it all the more surprising that he's the one that said, *"Act isn't just 'suddenly have magic.' There's physiological and biological changes that supports magic and your mana tolerances."*

*"He's exactly right,"* Takite said. Almost sounded proud, though I don't know why someone'd sound proud of this shit further making life hell.

Rotanu sighed — how'd that even work when he had no body? None of this made fuckin' sense. *"Ain't you can't get hurt. Can assure you, pain's still hell'va real and death ain't off the table. It's just increased healing for what you're talking; they've barely been burns to begin with, so you've naturally healed through 'em. Also why you keep having random energy spikes — that healing's coming from somewhere."*

Hearing Thomas come inside from wherever he'd been, I took a deep breath. This conversation ain't over. Now that someone else's home, though, I couldn't continue it here. Sliding my sneakers on and grabbing my keys, I left, not bothering to lock the door — was Thomas's problem.

There's barely anywhere private in this damn city. Previously, I'd go to the library when I wanted to be left alone, but couldn't go there and talk to myself, so that's shot to hell.

The only place I could think of that's truly alone's the damn place it all began: that forest, still abandoned after Siani killed that bitch-brat and dozens of bodies'd been found a day or two later. They were still trying to figure out what happened there last I'd heard, but since no further attacks had happened, it'd shifted down the list of priorities to a more passive investigation. At least, that'd been what my classmates said they heard on the news; didn't know myself since we ain't got a tv.

*"Where're we...?"* John asked. At least I had my thoughts to myself. Only once — that time on Saturday with Kylie and Siani — had Rotanu taken physical control of my body. Otherwise, the *"older me"* just talked to the *"other incarnations."* Almost a comradeship. Nothing like me at all.

*"The park? But why?"* John pressed. He and Rotanu'd talked 'bout weapon types for over two hours today, particularly sword classes. I ain't in the mood to hear his voice any more than I already had, even if he generally pissed me off less than Rotanu. They all pissed me off less than Rotanu.

I kept walking. As expected, no one's here: it's a Wednesday at 6pm. Normal families were fixing dinner, spending time with each other. Doing whatever normal families did. It wouldn't be dark for another two hours though, so I had time to be alone and get actual answers for shit I didn't even know was being hid an hour ago.

Rotanu was uncharacteristically silent the whole time: no joke, no sarcasm, no casual conversation with the others.

I went to where I'd destroyed trees and grass. Remembered the location perfectly, found the still charred grass blades. The bark'd since melted, but it'd been fucked up for sure and was prob'ly dead b'fore long. Grass'd definitely seen better days as well.

I was done with this shit: balling my fist, I said, "What else do I need to know? What *else's* getting hidden?"

*"Nothing was 'hidden.' What, you want an instruction book? Like you'd read it."* Rotanu's as unhelpful as ever.

"What else should I know right now? Takite — you said manipulation or something? What's that? And what else's different with my body? Rotanu, you said 'one' of the changes're 'healing,' which means there's more."

Why'd I no longer even feel human? Like some bizarre alien in human skin. Pretend. Even more of a freak than I'd ever known.

*"How'd you remember exactly where this was?"* Rotanu asked. "I just... did."

*"One've your answers right there: memory's changed, hypermnesia's your ability. Got off a hell'va lot easier than Kyle — Kylie."*

Ability? Hyperwhat? I couldn't even say the damn thing, let alone do whatever the hell it was. "You made me murder a big-ass section here. Nothing special 'bout remembering where it happened."

Takite jumped in, a slight cough as he did so; given I seriously doubted he could get sick, it must've been to deter Rotanu from replying. *"Every mage has an ability. It's a unique skill that manifests after they begin using magic. Yours is memory related, I'm guessing by Rotanu's questioning."* Great, add more things wrong with me: something'd changed with my memory, something I couldn't even decipher or know the damn meaning of. *"And I don't think any of us intended to hide anything..."*

*"Oh, I'm hiding things. I wanna watch this shit show,"* Rotanu said.

*"I'm sure Rotanu doesn't mean that,"* Takite said slowly, a lower tone to his voice. Rotanu's ass got in trouble, and it made me smug in a way I hadn't been since I blamed shit on Thomas and got away with it as kids. *"Regarding your second question, I can't precisely recall all that has and hasn't been said, but I don't believe your mark, uhm. The direct translation from Riyatian is symbol, but ah... I guess it'd be close to what's referred to as a 'birthmark' here."* Birthmark? I ain't ever had one. Was Takite just making shit up to entertain himself?

Rotanu interrupted with a bored tone in his voice, *"Left upper hip. And protect it like fuck."*

Promising. 'Specially when no one jumped to argue or chastise or otherwise imply Rotanu's fuckin' with me. Gritting my teeth at the reminder that I hadn't ever had a damn shower in peace my whole life, which's *great* to find out *sixteen years in*, I bit the obvious bait on how these strangers knew my body better than myself. "Why the fuck not?"

No immediate answer, not even from Rotanu. He was the first to crack, giving an irritated sigh. *"Fine, fine, my fault. I'll do the honors."* Absolutely promising. What shit show was this? *"It's the focal point of your mana. Like I said, you can get hurt, but takes mana to heal whatever got fucked even if you don't specifically use a healing spell. So if that mana supply gets disrupted, you're dead. Short version: don't fuck around with it or you'll find out."*

"Wait, wait, wait. You can't just... just drop shit like — fuck..." How often my father beat my ass, how'd this even work? Glancing around, I saw I was still the only person in the forest, at least where I was here. I moved clothes off the spot Rotanu said, seeing nothing until... a small dot, not even a fraction of an inch, but it'd never been there b'fore. First glance, it looked just like a birthmark, but the coloring's wrong — it's actually dark red and blue, just so small it's barely noticeable. The tip of my pointer brushed against it, and a jolt of electricity shot through me, not quite painful but left me suddenly breathless.

*"To answer your question..."* Rotanu didn't sound annoyed for once. Almost amused even. *"It has to be broken. Will hurt like fuck if it gets bruised around there, but not lethal. So just keep the pointy objects away and you're fine."*

Fine, my ass. I didn't want this, was weird enough. And yet... what choice was there now? Rotanu wasn't lying 'bout this part; that much's obvious. Instead, I was an impostor of a human, a mimicry, and there ain't a damn thing I could do 'bout it.

# Chapter Twenty

## only human

Rotanu | May 25
Training House

It's too damn late, and this felt sketchy as fuck. Yet here I was, walking the familiar path to what barely qualified as a building when I'd rather my ass be in bed under normal conditions, let alone whatever my current state qualified as.

Dmitri yawned, a sleepy tone to his voice as he asked, *"Where are you going anyway, Rota?"* He's just waking up; his sleep schedule confused the fuck outta me but wasn't my problem either.

"A favor, even if I'm already regretting it." No one was around, so I could "talk to myself" all I wanted for once.

*"To... she goes by 'Sia'?"*

"Sorta. It's... complicated." I hated not calling her Kyle, like I had for years now. I had to go by "Rotanu" 'cause it'd make things confusing as hell to call me and the current Jordan by the same name. But this Kylie didn't go by Kyle, not yet. There's no confusion with calling my fiancée Kyle and the her of this time Kylie. Two different names. That said, no one else's jumping on that bandwagon with me, and she ain't helping enforce it either.

I opened the rusted metal door, giving it that normal shove

forward at just the right time. How many damn apartment doors'd been like this, where they near needed sweet-talks just to fuckin' open? That said, this one's exceptionally bad as always, requiring a bit more force than I was used to — "Jordan's" lack of upper body strength fuckin' with my perception of the force needed to open the damn door. Understandable, but still frustrating as hell.

Door open, I stepped in. Only one of the lamps're on; it's in the far right corner, away from any of the windows that shone moonlight in. I closed the door behind me, walking over to the lamp's location, where a very familiar woman sat with her back against the wall, eyes closed, knees pressed to her chest and arms around said knees. I didn't need to ask which of them sat there; instead, I plopped beside her, my back also against the cool brick wall, legs crossed into each other. "'Sup to want me out here in the middle of the damn night?" Her body swayed to leaning against my side, head against my shoulder. My head lowered to on top of hers, wrapping my arm behind her. "Kyle?"

She's in the body of the current Kylie, much like I was in the body of the current Jordan. 'Cause of that, her voice was a little softer than normal as she whispered, "I missed you."

"Yeah but like... ain't this a bit uh. Wrong? To sneak 'em out in the middle of the damn night, 'specially since it's coming out of their body's mana reserves."

"I'll offset it. It's fine."

"That didn't answer my question."

She huffed. "Whose side are you on here?"

"I'm just saying's all."

Her head lowered slightly, pressing into me further. "I just... needed a minute. To not be 'Sia.'"

"Rest're asleep?"

"Besides Leah. But that doesn't bother me as much as what I need from 'Kylie' and a lesser extent from 'Jordan.'" I felt her tense, just for a moment. Was enough of a sign that something's indeed wrong; I kissed the hair by her ear. "And I don't want... They're not ready for us to just... be us. It's different than with the other incarnations, they're not them. You and I represent a future neither of them are ready for, and that's... that's okay. That's their right, to not want someone telling them tomorrow.

To be told they'll fall exactly in line with expectations because their future is our past and that's what it should be. I just..."

It's the same damn thing as always: she pretended to be strong. To not care. To take every hit and feel nothing. Yet she did. She felt it all, had for years now thanks to her empathy.

*"I see so much of Leah in her right now,"* John said, interrupting any pretense that I was alone. Sure, I was against sneaking around, but I also would've appreciated the hint Dmitri seemed to have taken 'bout letting me have this moment. I knew what John meant though, a stubborn as all hell and past anything resembling healthy boundaries resilience that Chloé'd never had the opportunity to refine. That Kylie'd yet to refine.

"Yet again, you're still only human," I said.

"I really need to fix that one day. It's a rather irritating limitation," she said with a chuckle. "I forgot though."

"Hm?"

"How much you've changed over the years." I said nothing, wasn't exactly my favorite subject in the world. She didn't seem to expect otherwise, chuckling yet again. "Oh, don't even. This Jordan's actually a lot cuter than I remembered. He's just trying his best. Give him that?"

Had her damn empathy active, and I should've known it; there ain't a chance in hell she wasn't full reading me with us having physical contact. "Kyle..."

"What? It's true. You don't get a vote."

I poked her rib with my finger, feeling the slight traces of fat that'd be replaced by muscle in the years to come. "Okay, first off, you know that ain't what I meant. Second, no, and not taking opinions on it."

She moved her hand over mine. "Yeah, yeah. You're the world's most unbiased judge here, I got it." I opened my fingers for hers to slide in. "You know, for a moment... I can almost pretend we're back home. That this is just normal."

"I know." I had nothing else to say. Touch, intimacy, validation were all I could give. I wanted to reach down and kiss her, hold her tight, hell, make out even. I knew better, though. It wasn't the time, the place. This's the best we had and even it's sketchy as fuck.

I was surprised Leah's allowed to see this side of her, that she accepted any of my own incarnations outside of the current Jordan might see her vulnerable. That her concern wasn't her pride but our younger selves' sense of agency.

My younger self's a fuckin' coward that didn't take responsibility for a damn thing that ever went wrong; I didn't give a damn 'bout his feelings 'til he learned what a spine was.

I thought back to right after my Act — when I was this "Jordan," what I remembered from Kylie then. She didn't trust "Sia." Well, she didn't trust any of the previous incarnations to be fair, but Sia's particularly suspicious. It's a very typical Kyle strategy: place herself at arm's distance to manipulate the responses people gave her. "Your aim's what I assume?"

She tensed, didn't seem to care for that question. I doubted even my other incarnations took notice of the gesture, though — that's something I'd worked my ass off to memorize. "My aim's never changed. My loyalty's always been to my Jordan."

If she meant what I thought that meant, she'd allow hell to happen, and I hated the fuck outta it.

# Chapter Twenty-One
## confusion, longing, concern, and...

Kylie | May 27
Rae Residence

Finals were over. This should've been the one time in the year I got to relax, just be a teenager. I hadn't even pretended that was an option, and unfortunately, that instinct had been spot on: no homework just meant more magic work. Today was a prime example: Mom was at work and was going to be gone all day since she had staff meetings after her normal summer classes. When I could've been hanging out with friends, maybe even having a pleasant lunch at the new cafe that opened last month, I was instead in my living room. Jordan awkwardly sat on the couch away from me, and I hated I knew exactly how awkwardly it was because yet again, emotions swarmed me.

"Okay, so we're both here," I said. Sia had a plan, and that generally meant trouble for everyone involved.

*"Can I take over for just sec? I need to tell Rota something, and it's easier than trying to relay back and forth."*

I nodded; I wasn't sure what it said about the state of my life that I had become accustomed to sharing a body with other souls. While I would've preferred they not be there, and I would've preferred that none of this happened, it had become almost a new normal. And while I didn't trust Sia, I also recognized I couldn't afford to not trust Sia; the one day that Sia was out of commission, I almost was kidnapped, was saved by Rota.

Sia gently pulled me from control of my body, where I became an observer of every movement, dulled yet present. I somehow saw Leah standing away in the blackness of the subcon; Chloé sat on the blackness despite no chair or anything; Kisate had her arms crossed over her chest, silent but very there. I saw all of them plus the muted sensations from my body at once, like a double vision, only Sia absent as the one in control of my body. "Rota, I'm going to release what she has active at the moment. It's nowhere near what you're used to with me, but still, be wary because there's going to be double the information incoming."

Jordan's eyes drifted down to his lap. "He asked if there'll be kickback on you for it."

Sia didn't immediately provide an answer. A few moments, she said, "I don't think so. Not enough at this point, at least. It's like 105-110% maybe so the slight increase shouldn't be anything unless a premonition kicks in."

Olive-brown hair swayed as Jordan nodded. "He said okay."

*"What are you both even talking about?"* I asked. Why wasn't Jordan asking questions? Rota was concerned, and I didn't want to be remotely around anything that needed concern. I wanted to scroll through social media all day or go back to looking at colleges I might apply for in the next year, something I hadn't had the time to do since all this started. Magic had consumed every moment of free time I had.

Why was it my old life seemed kind of boring compared to now? It was safer, better.

Sia placed me back in control of my body; speaking of useful lessons, I'd really prefer her or Kisate to teach me how to do that on my own sooner than later. *"With your magic naturally increasing, not to mention the practices we've been doing..."* The practices had me near yanking my hair out — not because the magic itself was terrible. I would never admit it, but there was something thrilling about being able to create a small light that could illuminate a room out of thin air. About hearing Leah and Sia talk about hand-to-hand combat in a way that Dani had never so much as implied, like action stories out of a movie. Even about some of the culture and more so theory from Kisate and Sia that I had hated a month prior. Learning when it was no longer finals season was a lot less stressful.

The reason I wanted to yank my hair out was because of Dani. She insisted on learning every spell I did, and half the time, Sia left me on my own to teach her. While Dani may have been proficient in martial arts, she kind of sucked at magic. I had learned the light orb spell in about three hours. Dani took all weekend, and I was going to go back for round two tomorrow to see if she ever actually got it because the odds weren't high, and it was even worse because we weren't aligned somehow, and therefore the process was slightly different, but Sia still left me to flail and drown while Dani became increasingly agitated. Overall, those sessions just really sucked.

Oops. I had completely zoned out; at least it was on Sia and not Kisate — between the two, Sia was far more forgiving in that respect. "Sorry, what was that? Something about practices?"

*"Short version: more mana, more depth and range on empathy. Eventually, you'll need to handle all your reads without me, and exposure practice is unfortunately the best way to get more proficient. This is a safe space to practice since you can get more reads but it's not likely to overwhelm you."*

"Oh."

This was *not* going to be a fun practice *at all*.

Jordan glanced at me briefly before his eyes shifted back to his lap. "I don't understand what they're trying to say. Something 'bout 'ability' but why's that need me? From what I understood, it's a solo thing, not something you can share or..."

My cheeks grew red as I moved my eyes to the fake Persian rug Mom had in the living room center since what felt like before I was born. For not the first time in my life, I traced mental paths with the lines as I wished I wasn't in this situation. Sia wasn't offering to explain for me either. Kisate rarely took control of my body, and Chloé and Leah never did. If anything, all three had been pensive since Jordan's Act. Like there were words they wanted to say but couldn't. Their emotions had been confusing, but they had been consistently confusing, so I had tuned them out easier.

Meanwhile, from what I felt the one day Sia was unconscious, tuning anything out was about to be a challenge.

"Um. So, it sounds like Rota explained what abilities are?"

"Takite did, yeah."

The emphasis there showed Jordan got along even worse with Rota than with I did with Sia. It was kind of impressive, though I definitely wasn't going to say that to him. "For some reason, I have two. Even Sia doesn't know why, and from what Kisate, Leah, and Chloé have all said, they each only had one so it's... strange. But I have empathy and sensory precognition. The latter is like a premonition, but only through emotions and sensations — I don't see anything, and it's only happened once so far. Was a less than pleasant experience, so assuming you didn't get anything like it, that's a win." I kind of wanted to ask what Jordan's ability was; he had to have known if Takite had already talked to him about it. But Jordan had been even less enthusiastic than me with everything magic related, so I tried not to bring the topic up if it wasn't needed. "The former is what Sia wants me to work on: empathy. Um. It's like... feeling other people's emotions."

His eyes widened as anxiety flooded him; I felt what I had a sneaking suspicion would be the beginning of a very miserable afternoon as my own heart rate skyrocketed and a giant knot formed in my stomach. "Shit, like... all this time? Since March?"

I nodded. "It wasn't day one. Sia's been working with me on slowly gaining tolerance because it can knock me unconscious. The day you um." I knew the phrase: "Act." He knew the phrase. But I also knew better than to say it, not with how on edge he was. "When Rota saved me. That day. The reason it was so rough on me was because I had the full brunt of the empathic reads when Sia was unconscious, and by the end of the day, I was totaled." I winced, feeling his anxiety grow even more prominent, that knot twisting further. Anxiety... and pride? And sadness? And...

My fingers went to my temple, as if it would calm the

conflicting emotions flowing through me. It wouldn't, but I tried anyway.

Concern. "Kylie?" He reached forward, and —

Oh, I was falling. That's why he sounded scared. Everything was so loud. Confusion and longing and concern and —

"You could've warned me," I mumbled to Sia.

*"Didn't do it, actually — you did that one. Definitely not going forward until you stabilize though, you're completely correct there."*

"How'd...?" I could barely figure out my own emotions, let alone try to feel other people's. How'd I manage to go past the provisional limits Sia had set? I never wanted this emotional noise: not then, not ever again.

*"I'm guessing you subconsciously homed in on his emotions. Problem is, it's not just one set of emotions you'll get with him when you do that."*

That's where the conflict came: it was an emotion read from all the souls within Jordan's body. But even if that's the case, why had Kisate and Leah's emotions completely faded in comparison? It was like Jordan and those within him completely overwhelmed any other emotion reads.

Like that one day when Sia was out, and I couldn't place a super loud emotional signal I had. In hindsight, that had to have been Jordan, even though he was nowhere near the closest to me as far as physical location.

My eyes closed as my mind faded, overwhelmed by too much emotional noise and not even the capacity to make sure I didn't injure myself.

# Chapter Twenty-Two
## technical demonstration

Kylie | May 28
Rae Residence

I hated this summer break despite it just starting: yesterday with Jordan had been bad enough — he felt awkward the entire time. I wasn't happy with the idea of him being a walking emotion test either, weren't my emotions to know, wasn't fun for me to experience.

And yet, as Dani and I sat on the carpet between my bed and the pullout couch guests used, I almost wanted to go back to then: Jordan's emotions were loud, but Dani's were intense and made me uncomfortable, though I wasn't really sure why. Her emotions weren't louder than Jordan's, just...

*"What's Dani's alignment?"* Sia asked.

Pulling me from my thoughts, I instead yet again mentally asked why Sia wasn't just taking control and teaching both of us at once. Of all the times I wouldn't mind Sia taking control of my body, right then was up there. "Um..." Worse yet, I barely kept my own "magic stuff" straight, let alone keep up with someone else's. Dani stared at me, half glaring, impatient. I knew her frustration wasn't truly at *me,* but I felt the frustration as if it was. Dani stared straight at me since there was no one else physically in the room, further connecting the

115

emotions I experienced with the frown on her lips and a tap of her finger on her crossed arm.

I cringed as Dani said, "Well? What next? Why're we just *sitting here*? This is a waste of time."

"I, um. Sia's working through something with me, sorry. Just a minute more."

Dani was still not a fan of only hearing my side of the conversation, as if I could control who heard Sia, Kisate, Chloé, and Leah. It just... kind of worked that way, and Sia was significantly more hands on whenever Rota and Jordan were around, whereas with Dani, well.

Her supposed reasoning was that I needed to get confident and have a thorough enough understanding to teach the concept, and Dani was the perfect opportunity to practice. I suspected that Sia just didn't want to deal with Dani: first Dani got upset that I could use magic, heard voices. Then she got upset that she was a liability, that Sia had protected us both — demonstration of said voices and that Dani's years of training hadn't been the end all she had always thought, and that I had always thought as well, to be fair. Then Dani's hostility to everything increased to near suffocating levels once she found out Jordan used magic too and Rota existed like Sia, while Dani had no other selves or future selves.

I wished I could go back to normal high school conversations and complaining about homework or our parents or anything that wasn't whatever the past few months had been.

"Well hurry up," Dani said. "I need to catch up to you, and obviously will need to know more than whatever he learned yesterday."

Sia snickered, and I added another tally to my "I wish I knew how to remove myself from control over my body" count. I did it once that time in April and had never successfully repeated the act. I had even tried in bed, so I was safe if no one took control over my body if I succeeded. Yet again I tried to remember how I had pushed myself from control, and yet again I failed. Sia chuckled, more softly this time. *"Again, Dani's alignment?"*

"Why do I need to know? Isn't that her problem?"

Dani glared at me but didn't say anything. Yet.

*"It's yours right now. And it's fire. We'll run through the scan test again later."* Great, now I had more work after all this with Dani was over. Dani wasn't about to be the only one shooting mental darts with how this evening was shaping up. *"And yourself?"*

"Um..." It felt awkward to say any of this out loud, especially with someone else physically in the room. But I knew, had felt an increased awareness ever since my Act, even before Kisate had confirmed it: the wind spoke to me; water calmed me. "Air and water."

*"Good."*

"What about them?" Dani asked. She was trying to jump into the conversation, and yet again, why wasn't Sia in control? I slouched to make myself smaller. It wouldn't do anything, but I wished it would.

"Um. Sia was asking about elemental alignment, and I was just answering... I'm sure she's going somewhere with it. Quickly."

"That's wrong then," Dani said. Oh no. Here she went again. "You just said two — that's not you and me, because *Sia* said fire before."

"Oh, um, it's just mine. I need to review over the spell for checking other people's again. I'm not doing something right, but it's whatever. Can work on that later."

Dani's head shook, red hair swaying with the gesture. "Then what's my other one?"

Sia said nothing, and I further attempted to distance myself from my body — I'll take a concussion over the brewing storm that was Dani's emotions. Sia sighed. *"We'll do a technical demonstration of basic healing magic. I'll take over."*

Finally, some way I could run away from this problem. I nodded, not a second later Sia swapping control from myself to her. "We'll hold on that for a bit. I want to show how to use restorative magic, particularly a basic healing spell."

That was an entirely too smooth sidestep; Dani even fell for it. "Wait, you know how to...?"

Sia looked at Dani. "Sia, not Kylie. She can't teach what she doesn't know."

And there went Dani's mood back into anger territory.

Standing, Sia held her left hand out; she gripped Isare, the bladed staff I would one day learn to use; how Sia summoned the weapon with no spell, I wasn't sure. Sia then said, "Isare, form modification: knife." A knife replaced the bladed staff in Sia's hand; I could feel the same pulse of energy — of my mana intrinsic in the weapon, no matter its form. What I wasn't expecting was for Sia to turn my right arm over and slice across skin, a faint stinging I could still detect, blood dripping across my arm from the incision.

*"Hey, like, what gives?!"* I gave her permission to teach something, not hurt me.

"H-hey, you can't — how dare you hurt her!"

Dani was even angrier than me; it wasn't her body currently stinging and bleeding.

"Calm down, both of you." Sia chuckled. At most, she sounded amused, not remotely threatened. She softly placed the knife onto her leg, preventing the blood on the blade from touching more than skin. "You can't heal if something isn't injured." She laid her left hand over her right arm, an aquamarine fused with clouded blue-gray color generating around her hand: an aura, from what I had learned. The pain stopped; when Sia's left hand lifted, there wasn't even a scratch. "More serious injuries will scar, but something that minor won't be noticeable. If you learn one spell, that's the one you want to learn. It's the one that might literally save a life assuming it's used correctly and in the right potency."

Dani reached for the knife; Sia slapped her hand. "You don't get to use the sharp objects until you can heal whatever damage you cause."

That didn't stop Dani, her hand tightening around the grip. As Dani brought the knife closer, as if to inspect it, Sia rolled her eyes; the knife vanished. "W-what the fuck? *How*?"

"Didn't I just tell you 'no'?"

"If you're *Kylie,* then if she can do it, so can I. Especially if *he* can do it, then I damn well better be able to — give that back!"

Sia took a deep breath, and while I felt no emotion spike from her, I would've sworn said deep breath was from a test of her patience. Patience far beyond what I frequently received.

A knock at my closed bedroom door. Sia said, "Come in!" as

if nothing was happening, as if we were just talking while sitting on the carpet, as we had done so many times growing up.

The bedroom door opened; Sia turned her head to the entrance, seeing my — well, our, to be technical — mom there. "I'm about to go pick up dinner. Getting pizza. You girls want the usual?"

A nod, slight smile. "That'd be great. Thanks, Mom!" Sia was too good at passing as me; I hated I knew Leah couldn't, Kisate couldn't, Chloé couldn't. It was something that further proved Sia was who she said she was.

Mom closed the door back; there was the distant sound of the front door opening and closing a few minutes later.

"Kylie?"

Sia turned her head back almost instinctively. There was a pause before she said, "Not yet. But soon, we just need to finish what we were working on for the basics of this healing spell."

Of course, that was when I was suddenly back in control of my body. I made a fist with my right hand and confirmed there was no indication of the previous injury.

"Well?" Dani said, impatient as ever.

*"First you learn, then you teach to her."*

That was easier said than done, and Sia had to have known it. Taking a deep breath herself, I said, "So, like?"

*"Center your mana and draw on it as we've previously practiced."*

"Give me a second, Sia's teaching me first so I can relay to you."

Dani crossed her arms over her chest. "Why doesn't she teach us both at the same time?"

Same question both of us had asked more than once now, and it felt every bit as valid as the other times. I wouldn't win the fight; Sia would avoid the question, and there were too many other fights I had with her to make this my hill to die on. That was rapidly changing, given the annoyed mood radiating from Dani, however. There had yet to be an instance where empathy had benefited my life; it was better than the sensory precognition, but that's because the one sensory precognition episode I'd had was up there as one of the most miserable things I'd ever experienced, and that was saying something given my life had rather sucked the past many months. "I'm not sure."

*"It's because she's not the one whose life depends on knowing this, yours is. She's just here because she insists on being here, so might as well make her useful."*

I sure wasn't repeating *that* back to Dani, so I instead did as Sia instructed: I stared at my hands, eyes unfocused on anything specific. Stilling my breath, I found the warmth of what Sia had called my *mana*, the same type of warmth constantly emanating from the ring resting against my heart, tucked under my shirt. I saw a glow around my hands: my aura based on what I'd been taught so far.

"W-what?" Dani jumped back, ever so slightly, before drawing closer, as if inspecting my hands. "It's like when she just... but *how*?"

*"Where you cramped your hand the other day? Lay your other hand over it and will it to mend. It's typically not even worth healing but works for this exercise so Dani doesn't go into panic mode with an actual injury."*

If I hadn't been focused, I might've snapped something to the effect that not being injured was, in fact, a good thing. But instead, I did as Sia said, laying my right hand over my left lower palm. A refreshing sensation pushed through where the cramp had been, as if disintegrating it. My heart raced — I couldn't tell if it was from the rush of gathering and actively using magic, still such a foreign and surreal experience, or if it was my body responding to the healing magic I had just used. "Wow." Sia was correct in that it was nothing compared to the cut Sia had healed, but still. It was my first practical spell, or at least more practical than the light orb.

*"Now when you teach Dani, you need to start at how to center herself and gather mana."*

Sia wasn't wrong: that was the foundational step for all magic usage, or at least conscious magic usage. "So, um. You want to like..." How could I describe this? It was an internal warmth. "Really focus, but relax."

Dani raised her eyebrow at me, and I knew it wasn't exactly undeserved. "How do I do that?"

It wasn't fair that I was teaching Dani this way when Sia had relaxed my body to the ideal resting state by having partial control when teaching me how to gather mana. Meanwhile, I couldn't exactly do that for Dani. "Um. You want to really slow your breathing, and then like, find this warmth. Mentally grab hold of that."

While I expected more push-back, Dani closed her eyes and took in a deep breath. "It's like a meditative state. I can do that easy." Dani's emotions did steady, center. A calm I didn't know Dani could have, especially not so quickly. "So?"

"Do you feel that warmth?"

"Not anything unusual for a meditative state, no."

That was not what Dani was supposed to say. Once I was centered, it had almost been instinctual. "Like... like your absorption device. That kind of warmth."

Dani's dark brown eyes opened, a stare at me. "My what?"

"You kn — " Dani obviously didn't know, actually. "It's like my ring or your... it's your earring, right? The left one?"

Dani's fingers, nails painted with black nail polish, went to her left ear. "Oh, this thing. Yeah. What's her name said I'd be fucked if I took it off."

*"Can confirm, she would indeed be fucked,"* Sia remarked, clearing any suspicion that she had been the one that Dani referred to.

Reaching for my own absorption device, I lowered my eyes to the beige carpet. "Don't you feel like a warmth from it?"

"No shit, it's been in my ear for weeks. Body heat."

"Not that kind of heat, like... something more... internal. Intrinsic."

A pause, Dani genuinely taking a moment to try, to be serious about my instructions. She huffed a few seconds later, shaking her head. "Nope. Nothing. Why're you making this so hard? Your teaching sucks. Maybe Sia should be the one to instruct me."

Sia chuckled; I wished she would take control back, but she didn't. *"It's not your teaching — well, it is a little bit, but you're still learning yourself. It's more of that she's not naturally attuned like you are, which she was very warned about, and said she didn't care. She's just not gifted in magic. More like the reverse, so of course you're going to be naturally more skilled. Just the way of things."*

Yeah, completely and totally did not help my situation of

having an annoyed and frustrated friend on my hands for the rest of the night. I hoped Mom got back with that pizza soon because I needed an escape starting about ten minutes ago, and it had yet to come.

# Chapter Twenty-Three

## that's enough

Jordan | May 29
Boyle Residence

It felt like no one else in the entire damn house ever bothered to pick up a damn thing or even attempt to keep shit clean. I was yet again scrubbing the counter with a used sponge, trying to clean shit I heavily suspected's Thomas's fault given it's marshmallow paste, and only he could stomach the raw sugar in that shit. The counters in this particular apartment're white. Or were white at one point in their life, was more of a yellowish-white now 'cause they're prob'bly older than me. Further pissing me off're the nits in the top covering that're perfect for crumbs to get stuck in and annoy the living shit outta me.

I needed to clean this whole damn house 'cause at least then it blocked out the shitstorm of yesterday, where I was a damn emotional open book to what had been my only friend for years. I caused her pain, and wasn't even trying, and it'd been going on for fuckin' months, but I hadn't noticed. Rotanu'd even known what's fuckin' going on and hadn't said a damn thing.

She wasn't supposed to know how I felt. Wasn't supposed to deal with my fucked-up brain, was better than me. The sidelines're enough. Just being around her's enough.

I needed to scrub harder. Damn stain's still there.

"Jordan — your turn for dinner. Get on it: should've started half hour ago!" Jewel yelled. Everyone else's damn useless, making it where only we could cook yet again: Elaine'd just eat snacks and not bother, Thomas's taste palette sucked and always overcooked *everything* somehow, and I wasn't sure if my father'd ever touched a stove in his life. Or anything 'sides the fridge to get a beer, for that matter.

Grumbling, "Yeah, 'prince' my ass, more like damn servant," under my breath, I walked over to the cardboard box with half the stable goods still in it; me and Jewel didn't see the point in unpacking more than the bare essentials when we rarely made it more than six months b'fore getting kicked out. How many damn times'd it been now that everything we owned's in Father's shitty-ass pickup truck and had to deal with finding our own place to sleep 'til Father got another "permanent" residence. I didn't even bother changing home addresses at school anymore. There wasn't a damn point and getting him to sign any paper's hell anyways.

All this's just another piece of proof that me being involved in all this magic shit's a mistake. Someone like Kylie made sense, born to be special. But me?

Yeah fuckin' right.

"Jordan!"

"I'm starting right now," I called back; needed to get started b'fore she got on my ass more than normal. Would be nice if she'd be in a non-bitchy mood for once in her life.

I dug through the box for whatever looked easiest. It's a "put the least amount of effort in as possible" night.

*"Did any of you have siblings?"* Rotanu asked.

I rolled my eyes and wanted to ask who fuckin' cared, and why'd I hafta be stuck listening to them? I just wanted to, at the very least, *pretend* I was alone for one damn second.

*"A younger sister, Anna,"* Dmitri said. *"She was nine when, well. Things happened."*

Rotanu paused before saying, *"Sorry. That's a shitty topic to bring up, considering."* Rotanu apologizing? I needed to check the moon that night. Was gonna be goddamn blue. *"Most've my focus's been on Riyatian history, ain't had time to really go into other periods ouside've what school and shit's covered. But that's such a half-assed covering. Doesn't really tell you anything 'bout what* actually *went on."*

Why Rotanu cared to begin with, I couldn't fathom, truly didn't understand. It's yet another sign that whoever Rotanu was, he ain't me.

*"I don't even know how you got access to Riyatian history to begin with. Even in my time, nothing was around, let alone now,"* John said.

And yet again, they're having a damn conversation, like I wasn't forced to listen to them. Like I was in the way of them having a damn afternoon talk, and I was just the unfortunate third wheel in an aspect of my life I didn't know it'd even be possible to be a third wheel in.

*"There's plenty, just gotta know where to look."* That playful tone from Rotanu pissed me off more than if it had come from the others. The sheer idea that Rotanu could be me...

The sheer idea that Rotanu could be *happy*, and that Siani's a future Kylie, and they're a couple.

It's an infuriating lie. I was meant to be at the bottom of every totem pole, and I wouldn't be let down again. It's better than I could hope to even be friends with Kylie.

That's enough.

# Chapter Twenty-Four
## compatibility

Admittedly, I could've let them work from Kylie's house instead of the training house today: I had no plans for training either with practical application or even roping Rota into a few rounds of sparring, despite the idea sounding even more appealing than usual. Leah must've been up exceptionally late since she was still passed out, and Chloé was winding down for a rest period, leaving just me, Kylie, and Kisate awake on our side for this blast of a magic theory and concept lesson. I could discern Jordan and Rota's emotions along with two others that were from the Kaku Tiza line, but I couldn't tell which was which since I didn't know any of them outside of Jordan and Rota. I had control of Kylie's body while Jordan was in control of his own, us both sitting toward the middle of the living room section of the training house, cool concrete pressing into the bare skin of Kylie's jean shorts and against her bare legs. Jordan sat with his legs crossed, slightly leaning forward; he was in shorts, so at least I didn't need to sneak any healing today.

For not the first time, I envied Rota's hypermnesia: I wished I could remember how the "Sia" of my past started this conversation. Maybe I should've even asked him sometime before right now. Unfortunately, casual conversation with Rota was currently difficult, to say the least. It had been years since he and I talked so rarely, and I missed his companionship so much. As it was, this younger Jordan, so timid and exhausted and cautious, was a reminder of how proud I was of Rota.

That said, I also kind of wished Rota was the one in control so I could've tried to bargain some AC into this heat trap we were currently all in. The great thing about this training house was it was completely abandoned, but that also had the unfortunate side effect of no utilities, and thus, no AC while it had to be in the hundreds outside. I didn't want this conversation overheard, so I preferred here, but I was really questioning whether the risk justified the means here because why did summers suck so very much?

Taking a deep breath, I suppressed any empathic readings I had, something Rota often referred to as deactivating my empathy; that wasn't technically correct given I couldn't actually "turn off" empathy any more than people could turn off seeing or hearing or touch. It was a sense like those, and I could just adjust how much I focused on it. ...It just also wasn't worth correcting Rota for what must have been the thousandth time.

"We've got some fun today," I said.

*"I don't like your definition of fun,"* Kylie said.

"You and Rota both, but that's why I didn't ask."

"Uh? Should he...?" Jordan pointed to himself. While he wasn't yet the Rota I loved, he was still adorable, and Rota was completely wrong about Jordan having no redeeming qualities.

I shook my head. "Doesn't really matter to be honest. It's all stuff Rota knows, but this is more of my area than his, so better for me to explain."

Jordan almost had the makings of a snicker on his face before he quickly got rid of it, eyes shooting down to his lap as he tried to hide any sign of amusement. I knew exactly what that had meant: Rota had said something, likely about how *thorough* I was known to be. I rolled my eyes. "Rota, don't even start or else you'll get to be today's teacher instead because I *know* you remember what I'm going to talk about. And no, I don't need empathy, don't even."

*"Wait, you can hear Rota?"* Kylie asked.

"Not at all, just know him well enough." Another breath. I didn't want to talk about the downsides of magic and being a mage to two teenagers who didn't want to be mages but were past the point of return on that one. It had to be Rota or me though, and it was better I do it. "First matter of business is some foundational knowledge: we've discussed mana drain before, but the refresher on that one is if you're out of mana, you're dead. Where I'm adding on is mana transferring, where mana is transferred between mages. The overall concept is simple enough: mana from one mage is transferred to another, like a blood transfusion, and for most mages, that's it." But they weren't most mages, and that had benefits and detriments they'd be learning for years to come. "Like with blood, not everyone is compatible with everyone: specific elements themselves aren't important, though similar elements can increase efficiency. The important part is the *number* of elements being transferred. More is fine, but you can't receive less. Most people only have one element, but you're both the lucky recipients of *two* elements, thanks to the purity of linage."

*"Finally, some respect for the work that went into the royal family's —* " I didn't let Kisate finish. We'd be here all day on some linage rant if I did, and there were far more important things going on than whatever uncle she had that hadn't existed for two thousand years. Takite was supposedly significantly more reserved, and I really could've used that in my life.

*"Because* of that," I said. "You can only receive a mana transfer from someone else of similar number of elements. Of the people you both know, that totals each other. Not Dani. Not anyone else. Bad things happen if you try it." I wanted to go into exactly *what* bad things would happen, but Jordan was already pale. I wasn't sure if it was because Rota had indeed gone further, or if Jordan was just creeped out; either was pretty likely, and telling him it'd cause his body to reject the mana and severely injure itself with incisions because of trying to simultaneously absorb and erase the foreign mana because of the unclean conversion from a mono-element mana transfer, well... I doubt it'd improve his mood to say the least. I still had my empathic readings suppressed, so I wasn't exactly sure what Kylie felt, but her silence erred toward daydreaming again. No

matter, I knew how to wake her up right about now. "Furthermore, it bears repeating: almost every spell uses some form of mana. Your body uses mana to survive, having already forgotten how to operate without it. Run out of mana, you're dead, and it's not a pleasant death, let me assure you."

Kisate was likely sending none too comforting empathic reads right then, and both Leah and Chloé would've joined her if they were awake. I couldn't afford to completely suppress my empathy often, but it was one-hundred percent the right call today given I was feeling emotional temperature drops even without it. Some days, even I preferred not to get slammed with everyone else's hesitation and sorrow and whatever other things they pleasantly unconsciously shoved on me. My own emotions were enough. Just like with the next topic, I had my own thoughts, but I couldn't express them, not now. I couldn't afford to waver, couldn't afford to show any weakness. There was no choice: I would play my part perfectly.

I would protect that which I cherished most.

Jordan softly agreed, but I doubt it was to me.

There wasn't time for distractions; we were against a timer, and I knew it, every second precious. "One more topic to cover now, then you get to be free until this weekend." I couldn't even let myself tense, couldn't let my voice falter; Kylie would notice biological reactions like that. I blocked empathic reads on me, but she could feel my body language. I needed perfect serenity, no weakness or vulnerability. A complete facade. "Neither Chloé nor Leah died clean deaths, were murdered by the same person." Jordan's eyes widened; Kylie did the mental equivalent of shifting uncomfortably, drug out of her passive daydream rather starkly. "Kisate's former servant boy, Asuza, killed them. And he isn't stopping there, unsurprisingly. We know his ability, like hypermnesia and empathy: it's what we'll refer to as 'aura tracking.' How can his reach expand so far? Short version: he's cheating. He knows the physiological appearance of Kisate and seems to have a bounty out on bringing the Kaku Kiseti line to him alive. He keeps shifting locations to where we don't know where he's at, but he'll be able to track Kylie with increasing precision thanks to her magipoten growing and using at least Chloé's if not Leah's body as well for an aura reference point. Just gets more dangerous as time goes on, especially if there's any kind of a large aura spike."

*"Wait, but they died, like, literal centuries ago. How?"* Kylie's tone was a mix of curiosity, astonishment, and disgust. *"Shouldn't it have like...?"*

"Mana preserves it far past what a lower-magipoten body would. Even past that, he's intentionally keeping them around for when he *needs them* again, such as now." I sighed. "Really, the fact that he has the element of surprise, plus been building up magipoten so much longer, *plus* such a network of resources and it's at all a struggle for him just shows how inept he is. He's not a strong mage at all; it's just neither of you have much mana right now and it's a constant guessing game. For better or worse, Jordan's likely safe since Asuza doesn't care about the Kaku Tiza line, but he's certainly aware of Kylie's existence by now, if not her outright location yet."

"Don't you... don't you know if...?" Jordan asked. "Doesn't *Rota* know the exact...?"

I wished I could tell him to take a hint for why I brought this up with such intensity, or why I knew Rota wasn't making jokes right then. Both Jordan and Kylie needed to grow up, to learn, and I would do whatever it took to give them that opportunity.

Bringing my pointer finger over my lips, I shook my head: silence was my answer.

# Chapter Twenty-Five

## princes and princesses

Kylie | June 10
Rae Residence

Mom's schedule had always been kind of sporadic; while the technical position had changed over the years, she'd always been an English professor at Jenn Community College. I'd grown up with us eating separately during the evening, some type of work or computer in front of us. There was one day a month that didn't happen though: the last Saturday each month, where we made time for each other with cheap takeout and a movie, a moment when both of our schedules came together. Unfortunately, spring basically always one or two missed months since graduation ceremonies required extra effort from faculty members at the college, and I hadn't really been in a place to even miss the event from all the activity in my life the past three months. I was only really looking forward to it right then because it allowed for some sense of *normalcy* to return to my life, and I would take that any chance I got, even if it was a makeup session in the middle of June so still wasn't truly normal. It really was a wonder that Mom had noticed nothing so far.

"Okay," I said. Mom hadn't made it home yet with the movie. I unpacked the to-go Italian onto the never-used-for-dinner dining room table — garlic bread and Alfredo for me, a chicken parmesan for Mom. Said table still wouldn't be used for dinner either since we were going to eat in front of the tv. Really, we should've been called it the "homework table" since it was more often used when Mom graded papers or I had more books than I could fit on my desk to reference while studying or writing a paper. "Here's our agreement: you all will shut up for three hours. That's the agreement. The end."

*"Oh, movie night! What'd she get?"* Chloé asked. It was a reminder that every moment of my life *before* Act they knew too. They had been silent observers, blocked away from my consciousness. And quite frankly, that discovery had been the creepiest thing thus far, even surpassing watching Sia *kill* someone. They couldn't hear my thoughts, and they weren't empaths like me and Sia. But it was still entirely too much of an invasion of privacy, and I wished Chloé would've realized that given she must have experienced the same thing with Leah and Kisate.

Speaking of things I hated, I hated I knew *why* Leah and Sia both chuckled or laughed or something. Maybe a snicker. It was something where I knew for a fact that they were aware of the discomfort I felt from Chloé's obliviousness.

Pretending that, for however brief a moment, I believed I was a reincarnation of Kisate, however far-fetched that sounded... that meant my *previous life* would've been as Chloé. But I was nowhere near as dense as Chloé was. Nor was I as prideful as Kisate. Nor as morally loose as Leah, who had regaled exploits of air magic being incredibly useful for stealing, especially in crowds. And that wasn't even approaching the problem of *Sia,* the one I somehow related the least with: she had no qualms about being a bitch to get her way. With killing someone and having no hint of remorse.

With being Rota's girlfriend.

Hearing the front door open, I hissed, "Again, *silence.* Three hours."

I did *not* want to deal with empathy, plus trying to enjoy the movie, *plus* a running commentary I couldn't reply to. One conversation was more than enough. Maybe this could begin a new trend of "Kylie gets to pretend not to have other beings within her."

That'd be the dream, but also it wasn't going to remotely happen.

"Smells great," Mom said as she walked into the kitchen.

"Had just come out when I got there." We both took our meals and supplied half-watered down soft drinks to the living room. Mom slid the DVD in — I didn't know what she had grabbed from the rental store; we alternated between who picked up food and who picked the movie. Half-slamming the remote buttons, Mom turned the tv on. I saw some fancy cursive logo in gold lettering flash across the screen.

Oh no, I had heard about this one — some romance story set against a medieval backdrop. I should've known: Mom always ate these stories up. Tightly held her blanket during the tense parts, cried at the end. Tonight would be no different except that Mom's emotions would end up probably pushing me to the same regardless of my actual investment in the story.

Maybe movie night wasn't such a great idea anymore. Another thing empathy made miserable in my life.

Yet... Mom was exhausted, but excited. She had missed this; I had missed it too.

The two leads predictably bumped into each other just a few minutes into the film. Romance had never been my thing. Same as when Dani always asked if there was anyone I wanted to date or found hot — just not my thing. Closest had been —

Oh, the love competition came in earlier than expected. Mom leaned closer to the tv. "Where's this type of prince charming when you need him?"

"In Hollywood."

Mom playfully ribbed me. "C'mon, isn't there *anyone*?"

"No?"

There was a striking difference between suspecting Mom didn't believe me and *knowing* by Mom's mild annoyance that she thought I lied to her. "You know you could tell me."

"Mom, seriously, only guy I even regularly talk to's Jorda — " Oops. That was something I knew better than to say. I didn't even blame the whistle sound from Sia.

All of Mom's attention dropped away from the movie and onto me. "You know you shouldn't be around him. What do you even see in him?" This dance yet again; it happened every time I mentioned Jordan, especially as I'd gotten older. Mom didn't approve of Jordan, and a morbid part of me wanted to ask Sia how, if Sia really *was* a future me, and Sia and Rota really were *together*, that worked with Mom. Because there was absolutely no way I could see it working in my current future; Mom would've completely flipped out.

"We've been friends since like elementary school, Mom. And I've yet to stop getting good grades, regardless of what he gets."

Mom huffed before looking back at the tv a moment. Simmering, great. The annoyance from Mom was contagious, increasing my own agitation. "I've heard enrollment is up, so you might want to look at adding some extracurricular activities back to your schedule to help further bolster your chances at a good college. Might meet more friends that way too."

Sia snickered, and I would've done the same if it wouldn't have gotten me in more trouble; I instead bit back an eye roll at how not subtle the real motivation was. "I'll look into it. Also is that the same guy at the beginning?" That was completely distraction bait, and I prayed Mom would bite because nothing good would come with this conversation continuing.

*"I'm sorry, but I can't,"* Kisate said. I guess she actually had been trying to stay silent like I had asked. Go figure, I wasn't expecting Kisate to actually cooperate with my request. *"'Better' than the chosen candidate's line? The raw amount of power —"*

*"I know."* And now *Sia* was saving me? Truly was a day of surprises. *"But she doesn't. And honestly, it's probably better that way."*

# Chapter Twenty-Six

## counterpart

Even though I handled jack shit compared to Kyle, it still sucked ass I couldn't pass out on my own schedule. Always had to keep an eye open. My memory helped a shit-ton, but there's so much I missed or didn't understand as *Jordan* despite having near constant control over my body and the senses that came from it.

Whoever said "hindsight's a bitch" was unfortunately entirely too spot on yet again.

Jordan was out by our normal 8:30pm bedtime, and I wished I was too. Instead, I maintained a semi-active conscious state within the subcon so I could keep aura suppression and elemental manipulation under control if he started stirring too much while sleeping — last thing we needed's him setting the damn bed on fire. I heard light footsteps walk toward me — John. Neither Takite or Dmitri'd trained in any type of advanced combat, in that degree of spatial awareness that the steps had. Opening my eyes, I glanced up. "'Sup?"

"Can we talk?"

At least he's upfront; I could respect that, even if it's kinda obvious when he's directly approaching me within a subcon. "Sure. Something on your mind?"

John sat beside me. "I guess best way to say it's that your counterpart... is she all right?"

Had to be Kyle. *Always* was Kyle, the perpetual troublemaker. "Kylie? Or Kyle — sorry, *Siani?*" I asked anyway.

"Siani. Kylie is similar enough to Chloé especially and even Kisate. But Siani... her movements are more erratic. There's these... microaggressions almost. Little things she does to both Jordan and especially Kylie that don't make sense." John chuckled. "At least with yourself, it's obvious to be regret." I hated being an open book to damn near everyone, but it'd always been that way, even to *myself,* so it seemed. "Is she actually trustworthy? The time we have... I assume you know when it is considering your memory, but it can't be that far off now with how high her magipoten already is relative to the general population. Jordan's another key giveaway that'll draw *him* to this geographic area."

He ain't wrong on any of those assumptions. "Neither Chloé nor Kisate're ever in combat," I said. "At best, Kisate learned a bit of healing magic and a few defense spells. Chloé... her knowledge was less than even Kylie's right now 'cause Kisate, well. Kisate fucked up." It yet again pissed me off that she couldn't live and stay innocent; the two couldn't align, 'cause to be alive meant she needed fight. It's how Leah'd survived as long as she had; it's how Chloé'd been such an easy target. "You trust Leah?"

John furrowed his eyebrows together before slowly nodding. "Of course."

Taking a deep breath, I nodded. "She's as trustworthy's Leah. Stubborn as a fuckin' brick wall, self-righteous's all hell, and isolates herself nonstop. Hell, won't even completely tell me what she's over there scheming. But she leads and I support. Hardly a new concept, as you'd know."

I heard John shuffle to get a better look at me. "How...? I never told..."

A third presence: Dmitri waking up. I hated the modifications that forced me into being eternally exhausted at dusk and up with the sun. Understood why it happened and the benefit of it even; I'd never'd used it, unlike Kyle'd done with her equivalent, but still. It sucked, and I envied being able to sleep during the day when nothing's remotely going on except for the asswipe of a father being as obnoxious and useless as ever. Dmitri stretched and yawned, walking over. "Oh, meet up?"

"Just talking mostly." I still wanted my ass in bed, but even as grumpy as I was... I knew these moments were precious in and of themselves. A chance with the past, to better understand.

Maybe a way to even make amends.

Dmitri glanced around. "Jordan's asleep?"

Unfortunately, that sounded like the start of a shitty-ass conversation I wanted nothing to do with. John said, "Has been for a bit." Unless I approached him directly, Takite distanced himself from the other incarnations. It's different from how I'd heard Kisate was, how Takite was b'fore this incarnation cycle. Likely's guilt, and it ain't completely undeserved.

Sitting down cross-legged, Dmitri lowered his eyes. "So like, something's been going on that kinda... concerns me with him."

Unable to help myself, I asked, "Only one thing? I'm impressed, I got a damn near notebook at the moment."

"Wait, you've got things too?"

Dammit. In many ways, Dmitri's more of a headache to deal with than Jordan 'cause at least Jordan'd acquired a sardonic sense of humor that I still very much used. Like right there. Where it'd gone straight over Dmitri's head. "Yeah, but — . Never mind, what's up?"

Dmitri drummed his fingers against each other for a moment, a nervous gesture. "It's about that other friend — like I'm glad he finally got another friend outside of Chloé's next incarnation..." If Kyle ever heard herself referred to as such, she'd have such a massive bitch-fit I almost wanted to set that firework explosion off myself just to watch the carnage. Almost. Cleanup'd be hell, and that made it entirely too much effort. "But I worry... that older boy... Richard, was it? He's just ordering Jordan around, can hardly call what they have remotely mutual."

Chuckling, I shrugged. "Let 'em be. It's good for him to get more friends and expand his horizons."

# Chapter Twenty-Seven

## burning alive

Damn Rotanu started nagging hours early to make sure I ain't late; something 'bout not wanting "Kyle" — for whatever reason he called Siani that — riding his ass. It sounded like Rotanu's problem, but unfortunately, he'd made it my problem. So we were there at this dumbass "training house" early — easily twenty minutes early. And Rotanu's snipe that I had nothing better to do might've not been wrong but was completely uncalled for. Could've at least hid in the public library where there's fuckin' AC.

There's nothing to do in this damn house while I waited. Nowhere to sit besides the concrete and the remains of a kitchen island, maybe a kitchen counter at the very back, and it's hot as fuck. Kylie's house and the library're the two places I often hid during the hottest summer months, with the library winning out the older we'd gotten.

*"How'd the Nuueti line get up to third anyway? Since's so close to the fall, wasn't a ton of records on it, and previous entries suggested they weren't even in the running previous generation?"* Rotanu said words, and I effectively understood none of them. It was incorrect to say there's nothing in this house actually: I

**141**

still heard the *voices* in my head continue their conversation that completely omitted me. Yet again, I wanted to ask why there wasn't a way for them to do that without me having to hear every damn word said.

"*There's some variance between genes to be fair,*" Takite said. "*It wasn't completely unheard of as a jump. There were... well, there were rumors at the time, but I just can't believe His Majesty would've...*"

"*What? Had a mistress?*" Rotanu snickered. "*Hell knew half the nobility line came from a mistress at one time or another. Wasn't like Riyati's special there — entire backbone's dependent on bloodline. Fact Tanoti even got utilized that generation's the more unique thing.*"

"*You're... informed as ever, I see.*"

Rotanu's chuckle had a nervous edge to it. Why? Hell if I knew or even cared right then. I just wanted them to shut up and preferably let me go somewhere colder. "*It's just interesting as hell, honestly. Like, it's near universally removed from the other world cultures of its time because of the island geography and the inherent isolation the culture promoted, so what's consistent and what's different, and where that's coming from to influence the culture...*"

So help me if Rotanu didn't shut up, I was gonna bang my head against the concrete wall 'til I was unconscious and didn't have to hear this shit. I wanted Kylie to just *get there* to get things started, even if I knew her presence would've at most paused their conversation.

Hearing the door be pushed open, I let out a sigh of relief: *finally*. Something to distract Rotanu from going off on some tangent 'bout history or culture or whatever shit he's talking 'bout. Another indication we ain't the same: I didn't give a damn 'bout any of that shit, didn't have the time or energy to devote to anything useless like that.

Except, the person who entered wasn't Kylie or Siani, not that I could tell the difference between the two of them besides their physical forms. Taller than Kylie, Siani, or even myself, bright red hair, tomboyish clothes: someone I hadn't seen in months, Dani. The hell's she doing here? This wasn't her side of the city, to say the least. Had Kylie invited her? If so, I would've appreciated getting the damn memo.

...Not that she had an easy way to contact me, but still.

"Uh?"

Even Rotanu and Takite paused their conversation.

Her brown eyes narrowed on me. "You."

She stomped up to me so intently I tried to take a step back away from her, only to realize I was already against the wall. How'd she even know this place? It hadn't been an accident from how she'd walked over to me. She's taller and definitely more in shape, neither of which reduced the intimidation factor. "Uh? Hi?"

We weren't exactly close friends; she kinda got on my nerves, and I'd never been her favorite person. Only reason we ever interacted's 'cause of Kylie, but she wasn't there, and that made the moment even more awkward.

Actually, *had* I ever been alone with Dani? Besides moments where Kylie just left the room for a minute or two... not really.

"She seriously thinks *you* can do it? *You* could protect her?"

"Uh?" I had no idea what she's talking about: it's safe to assume the "she" in question's either Kylie or Siani, and more likely's Kylie given Siani needed no one... but when'd I ever say I could *protect* her? Why'd Kylie have said that as well? I regularly got the shit beat outta me; I couldn't even protect myself. Hell, me and Kylie're supposed to meet here to learn more of this thing I shouldn't've even known 'bout to begin with.

I wished I was in Dani's position, should've been in Dani's position: on the sidelines, cheering on the people actually meant for the spotlight. Fuck, Dani could have *all this* if she wanted it, wanted the voices that wouldn't shut the hell up, the new rules and changes to myself that I never asked for.

"That's all you can say?" She swung at me, fist colliding with my shoulder.

I winced — while the soreness that pulsed from my shoulder wasn't necessarily a *new* sensation, I definitely hadn't been expecting or bracing for the pain. I tightened my eyes. "Fuck..." I wanted to yell back, ask why the fuck she'd punched me. But I didn't, just bit the words down.

"You can't even dodge a simple punch. She's wrong. You *obviously* aren't fit for this."

I *agreed* with her; why's she acting like I didn't? Why's she acting like I wanted any of this? I wasn't fit for this.

There're more steps, the door opening again from the other side. "Dani...? Why are you here? I thought we were going to meet up tomorrow."

She spun around, as if I wasn't there. As if she hadn't just yelled at me and then socked me. "I just wanted to check this house out. I don't know why you bother here when my gym at least isn't in the slums."

"Yeah, but, um." Kylie's eyes flashed to me, and I didn't like that I suspected she already had empathic reads from me. Could she feel this pain? Was that a thing? Her empathy's confusing as hell. "It's a different type of training, needs a different type of environment."

"What, burning alive in this heat?" She ain't wrong with that one. Damn summers sucked ass. Not that I liked winter more — I could deal with the heat more than the cold. Always'd been that way.

"It's, um..." Kylie walked closer, setting her bag down on the concrete floor. "I don't want to ruin the actual nice stuff you have in there, though." Her eyes lowered a moment b'fore nodding. "Sia wants to get started though, so if you want to stay, that's fine, but it has to do with — actually." Kylie's voice lost the almost pacifying tone at the end, gaining more confidence. "What *are* we doing today? You're already working me tomorrow too, so this better be important."

Dani huffed before walking to the door. "Never mind, I don't want to deal with *her*. I'll just see you tomorrow." I wasn't sure if she slammed the door or if it just took that much force to close.

Kylie grabbed a water bottle from her bag and offered it to me. "I brought extras this time. You okay? Heat not getting to you, right?"

It's more that the unexpected punch'd knocked the breath outta me, which I guess'd made me flush. I didn't wanna mention it though, didn't wanna get involved in whatever the fuck just happened more than I already seemed to be.

"Thanks." I took the bottle, drinking 'bout a third. The water wasn't cold, more of lukewarm, but I'd been thirstier than I'd realized.

She grabbed another bottle from her bag, opening it b'fore drinking some. "Least I can do is give you some water when Sia's the one dragging us out here to die from heat stroke. Which she has no sympathy for, by the way." A pause before Kylie said, "What? Why would I blame Rota? It's not like he controls the stupid weather."

*"Tell her I said no, I know* exactly *where that damn line of reasoning's 'bout to go and I'm not a damn thermostat for her amusement."*

I wasn't sure what he meant by that — if he could adjust the temperature, why the fuck wouldn't he? Maybe I could get a response out of Siani, better understand how Rotanu could affect any of it. "He uh. Rotanu said no, that he ain't a thermostat."

A slight nod from Kylie. "That's by *choice*, too, unlike the rest of us here. And you are *not* convincing me that this house's too big for his current magipoten because I don't believe it. Too low expend rate." That had to be Siani; for one, I didn't know half of what she just said. No way Kylie would've been that *direct* either.

*"Oh, fuck her."* My cheeks further flushed from Rotanu's curse. No way in hell'd I'm saying that one to Siani. *"I'm dealing with this directly."* I wasn't complaining when I lost control of my body, despite Rotanu not asking like he was supposed to. There's something almost playful in this exchange, teasing and biting in a way I'd never dream of being with Kylie. "Listen here," he said.

A slight pull of Siani's lips — not quite a smile, not quite a smirk, but amused in a way I'd never seen Kylie be despite still possessing Kylie's form. "I'm listening. And melting, by the way." I didn't wanna admit how hot I found her tone right then. Wasn't mine to see, to hear.

"You could get a damn breeze going too but ain't gonna volunteer that? Why the hell's it always *me* stuck dealing with temp problems?"

Siani's eyes stayed on Rotanu's face as her hand touched Rotanu's — my — arm and lingered. Out of the corner of

Rotanu's vision, I could see a light color — *aura* — from where her hand would've been. The pulsing in my shoulder vanished.

I wasn't sure if Siani knew what'd happened, but she certainly'd noticed my pain. Had healed me, and Rotanu'd even seemed to catch on, them bantering back and forth as the healing magic took place. As Kylie'd likely remain unaware.

"Oh, the reason *why* I say Rota?" There was this coyness, confidence and security. It's hot as hell and confusing as fuck to see the behavior from my closest friend. Well. Supposed older version of my closest friend, but still, it's Kylie's body. And she ain't on the table. Not that anyone was, but she 'specially ain't. Siani chuckled, eyes running over Rotanu's body — my body, even though Rotanu's in control, leading me to feel self-conscious 'bout what exactly she saw; did I forget to patch up somewhere on my jeans? Or something wrong with the shirt? Or — "It's a side effect of his particular element alignment combination: he can heat and cool enclosed spaces up to a certain size. Can confirm, he *definitely* could take the temp down like 15 degrees if he wanted."

"You know the shit-ton of mana it'd take? He ain't got..." Rotanu signed, shaking his head. "Fuck you."

"I'll spare them a response to that, but you know what I'd say."

I didn't particularly care for the almost snicker that Rotanu had. "Answer's still no."

"Killjoy."

# Chapter Twenty-Eight

## serious

When Sia had first suggested that Dani instruct me in martial arts, I thought it'd at least be a bit more time for us to hang out. Something normal in my life.

In hindsight, maybe magic wasn't so bad if it at least wasn't *chastising* me every single thirty seconds. I had never seen this side of Dani and could've quite happily gone my entire life without doing so.

Dani huffed as she grabbed my arm and jerked it back an inch. "Quit moving your stance."

"I'm not trying to." Forgive my body not enjoying being pressed into positions it wasn't exactly familiar with. Like right then, when Dani wanted my back left leg directly behind my front, arms not at all supporting me. It was supposed to help me work on balance or something. I didn't remember or frankly care right then. Physical training with Dani was better than magic training with Dani, the latter of which was scheduled after lunch. In other words, this was supposed to be the peaceful time of my Thursday.

"You need to take this seriously."

Relaxing to a more comfortable position, I crossed my arms

**147**

over my chest. "You really think I'd be in your gym of all places during my nice summer afternoon if I wasn't?" At least Sia restrained more of my empathy than normal to help me focus. Small blessings, especially with Dani in this type of mood; I had annoyed readings from I assumed Dani right then, but they were faint compared to how they could be.

"It's just really obvious you have no clue what you're doing. If this was a normal situation, I'd not bother and just protect you myself." She had no idea the amount of restraint I showed by not snapping back about how, if this was a *normal* situation, I wouldn't have been here in the first place. I was here because the past four months had demonstrated that things were, in fact, quite *not normal* anymore. "The fact that *he* 'protected' you shows just how much more practice you need."

Opening my mouth, I hesitated at how to even approach that hornet's nest of a statement. "Which 'he' are you even referring to? Because Rota — "

Dani rolled her eyes. "Like it matters. Same difference." The difference between Jordan and Rota was every bit as drastic as me and Sia, not that Dani would know given she avoided Sia as much as she could — which was understandable — and didn't acknowledge Rota even existed. I hated this topic that had come up again and again lately, where Dani's emotions made absolutely no sense. But it always led to her going off on Jordan when he wasn't even here. "That scrappy pipsqueak protecting anyone's a fluke, and we can't let it get to that again. Straighten your back up, next we're going to — "

"No." It truly was the same thing yet again. I was tired. He didn't deserve this.

I didn't deserve to be treated like this.

"What, you *still* need a break? Maybe stamina should be more of a priority since you're so weak-willed that — " Balling my fist, I turned around and walked to the bench in the corner of the room, where my shoes, phone, and overnight bag sat. "Where're you going?"

"I'm done."

Dani sprinted over, grabbing my arm. "No way, we just started. If you're *really* serious and don't want these things happening again — "

I wasn't the one who didn't understand; Dani was the one treating this like some side adventure. Ripping my arm free, I met Dani's eyes. "You're the one who isn't serious: this is some game to you. It's not your life being in danger constantly getting waved around in your face. *You're* not the one who has almost been kidnapped twice. *You're* not the one who might die. You're learning magic because it's *fun* for you. Because as you've all but said, it's *exotic*."

"What, you think you've got this all handled? That *he'll* save you?"

Sliding my tennis shoes on, I put my phone back in my jean shorts pocket. "First off." I turned back around to face Dani. "'He' has a name. It's *Jordan*. And I know you know this because I've known you *both* forever. Second, maybe Jordan can't, but *Rota* already has done a better job than yourself, who had to go get saved by Sia *and* almost caused a bigger headache. Like, you know how terrible it is I'd rather learn from *Sia* over yourself? *Sia*. So yeah. Screw you, I'm done."

I walked up the steps and out of the house; I'd rather study in that stupid AC-less training house than endure another moment of Dani's "training."

Dani called after me until the front door, but I didn't care. She didn't chase after me, and I was done.

# Chapter Twenty-Nine

## something familiar

Today's actually slightly better than the past few days, only "miserable" instead of "suffering in hell" levels of heat. It's a pleasant change, 'specially with the slight breeze rustling leaves from the nearby trees.

She's already waiting for me, sitting at the bench we always met at; it's first time in a while she'd mentioned wanting to hang out at all given how frequently we'd been together from imposed *training sessions.*

"Late as usual, I see," she chided as she glanced up from her phone screen.

I rubbed the back of my neck with my hand. Jewel wouldn't shut up yet again, so I couldn't get going like I wanted to. "Yeah, sorry 'bout that."

Kylie stood, stretching her arms out b'fore shaking her head, slight smile present. "It sounds weird, but... it was actually kind of nice." Placing her phone in her pocket, she started walking, me following her onto the walking trail we'd walked hundreds if not thousands of times prior.

"Just a bit, uh, strange."

She chuckled lightly before glancing at me. "It's just

**151**

something almost, I guess you'd say, familiar. Feels like one of the few things that hasn't changed."

One of the few things that hadn't changed, huh? I hated I related to what she meant, hated my family fuckin' up my ability to show up on time's so minor compared to the other things going on. Even more so, I hated whatever cosmic mistake had me involved in this shit at all: I wasn't special. At least not the good or even neutral kind.

I glanced around and saw one couple from our high school sitting on a bench not far off the trail. Both of them're typically in Kylie's honors classes if I remembered right. The girl with long blond hair sloppily tied up's leaning to the guy, kissing him on the cheek b'fore the guy pulled her onto his lap. I quickly glanced away, a blush filling my cheeks. Kylie didn't seem to notice them at all, her head down toward the cobblestone walking path.

She never noticed.

"Was surprised you wanted to hang out since the other day and all," I said. My attention needed to shift b'fore Rotanu got any ideas for a running commentary; it's already amazing he'd stayed silent.

She stopped walking, hand reaching for the ring she wore as a necklace pendant. The thing that we'd been informed's an *absorption device*. A method of storing surplus *mana*. My own was the necklace she'd given me on my birthday, barely a week b'fore everything started. It was terrifying to even consider my sanity's connected to a piece of plastic jewelry, but there's no doubt that *something'd* shifted with the pendant: it held a warmth to it that's intrinsic and beyond what would've been body heat.

Another set of classmates passed us, this time two girls. They giggled and whispered to each other while gesturing to me and Kylie with their heads. I overheard one saying, "Can't believe she still hangs out with that weird kid. Must be pity." The other voiced agreement.

I lowered my head. More of the same shit on a different day.

"Mm. I just..." A breeze shifted through the trees, blowing a few fallen leaves through the air.

*"See! Right there. Ain't just me."* Rotanu might as well've

been jumping up and down like some hyperactive brat. *"Dammit, it took a long time b'fore she slipped up while we're together. But dammit, not just me, and I called it."*

I rolled my eyes. I ain't interrupting Kylie's thoughts to comment on how Rotanu'd apparently waited for Siani to fuckup on controlling Kylie's elemental manipulation. But if I *had* been in the mood of replying, I would've noted that this's like the first time compared to Rotanu's at least once a week if not daily fuckups.

In fact, I still wasn't sure how Rotanu determined the breeze's unnatural 'cause it just felt nice, calm. I half wondered if he's bullshitting me, and maybe another time, I would've asked. Not right then though, with her standing there, eyes focused on the pathway b'fore us.

"It's been a while, you know?"

"Uh?" I completely didn't know what she meant.

Almost glassy aquamarine eyes met mine, a brilliance to them that caught my breath. "Since you... since Rota saved me, we've been around each other more, but it hasn't really been on our terms. I just... wanted to... I don't know." She chuckled as she moved her eyes away. "Sorry, I'm just making this more awkward. You've probably got better things to do, and I'm just confusing you, and — "

I hated she knew my emotions just like I hated I couldn't stop my newly enhanced memory: *hypermnesia,* according to Rotanu. "I-it's okay. Nothing really going on anyway."

She nodded, but her eyes grew glassier. She sniffled b'fore it progressed to a choked gasp. I didn't know what to do; I watched as first one tear, then two, then four tears slipped down her cheek.

Rotanu sighed. *"Fuck's sake, what're you even doing you dumbass?"*

"I don't..."

Thankfully, I was quiet enough that she didn't notice and instead wiped her eyes with her arm b'fore she said, "I'm... I'm sorry," between disheveled breaths.

Rotanu took partial control, something I didn't even know's possible. He closed the distance between us, holding her and patting through her hair. He then released control, leaving me in the most awkward as hell position I'd ever been in. Even though I wanted to complain, I didn't 'cause she leaned her head against my shoulder as she choked out additional words between strained breaths and sobs. "I'm scared. I'm so scared."

At least no one was nearby, finally.

I clumsily continued stroking the top of her hair — so soft, like silk, watery strands slipping through my fingertips. I felt her pressing into me, and even despite the seriousness of the moment, I struggled with remembering my emotions're an open book to her, so there're thoughts that needed to wait 'til I was *far* away. Emotions Rotanu'd give me hell over later, and that's bad enough; I didn't need her asking and makin' shit even more awkward.

But.

Even more than the potential embarrassment, I hated she's this terrified. There's nothing I could've done: I ain't strong, ain't impressive. "You'll be okay," I said. "You're strong. You'll get through this."

# Chapter Thirty

## to die, again and again

Siani | June 20
Subconscious Principality

June was almost over; it had to be soon. Rota would know for sure, but I couldn't really ask him without some really obvious giveaways. I wanted to take control of Kylie's body, ask Rota to do the same to Jordan. I wanted to sneak out again, have another *secret date*. But it wasn't safe. Everything — the weight of survival, of *existing* — depended on me not buckling; Kylie had long since done so, and that was understandable. It really was.

Chloé sat beside me, knees up to her chest and arms wrapped around her knees, an energy to her I envied. "Sia? Is everything okay?"

"Mm. Just tired. I might be resting here soon, been a few days at this point."

"'Days'?" Chloé's head tilted, shoulder length hair falling forward. "How d'you even do that?"

Forcing myself to lightly chuckle, I shook my head. "Lots of practice. It's easier without a body at least."

"You've never said how that works." Since when was Kisate up at this hour? *Her Highness* usually went to sleep before Kylie, or rather she pretended to be asleep and did her own thing; I didn't really care as long as she wasn't causing me further headaches.

"Mhm," I said.

"Just leave it," Leah said. She saw the challenge Chloé had predictably missed. The one that I didn't bite into for once. Where was my trophy for that? Granted, I didn't bother simply because I was genuinely exhausted, but it wasn't from a lack of rest, like I had told Chloé. Or at least, not *just* a lack of rest. I was trying to piece together my memories and all the actors at play, and it took more out of me than I wanted to admit. Or maybe it was dealing with empathy for both me and Kylie while stomaching sensory precognition attacks that I had shielded her from. The cause didn't really matter when the end effect was that Kisate was too much effort and a waste of my limited time.

"I refuse." Kisate might as well have stomped over to me, and I wasn't even sure how it was possible to *stomp* in a subcon. Like that was even more effort because it was further visualization of the self, and — "I want an answer. I've waited long enough."

I didn't bother looking up and instead closed my eyes as I leaned my head back, felt hair brush against my wrist. "Shouldn't be hard to figure out if you're as good as you claim."

Leah sighed, but for the record, that *was* the tame response. So help Kisate if I actually had the mental fortitude to waste on arguing with her.

"Why are you two always fighting?" Chloé asked. "Kisate, you never fought with Leah like this, even when you both disagreed..." She then shifted her attention to me. "And Sia, you get along fine with Leah and me. It's just Kisate..."

Kisate said nothing. I opened my eyes, seeing bright greenish-blue eyes peering at me. An innocence even my younger self no longer had.

I was envious, truth be told.

"Power," I said. It wasn't a secret. Leah knew, I knew, and Kisate knew: Leah wanted no stakes to power, preferring to watch from the shadows as she had in her life. Kisate was raised to command; I had survived by being a solo agent.

Chloé's eyebrows furrowed as she mouthed the phrase. "But

how? Why? Doesn't all the power route back to what Kylie has right now?"

"It's one of many questions," Kisate said. She must've been looking for that type of moment to jump in. "But that form you and *Rotanu* claim as your own respectively... it far surpasses what's possible right now." Did she think she'd figured something special out there? Of course it was; what other point was there in using our own forms if not for the extra simulation of mana they could pull as needed?

"Mhm." I wasn't directly confirming or denying anything to her, especially not right then. If she thought she was going to outwit me into admitting *anything* I didn't want to, well. Good luck. She'd need it.

"That's all you have to say?" Kisate's tone rose higher.

Finally raising my eyes to Kisate, I lifted my eyebrows. "If you wake Kylie up when it's the first night she's getting somewhat decent sleep all week, I will make *personally* sure you don't wake her up again."

"Is that a challenge? Do you not understand who I am?" Kisate's voice rose even higher, near to yelling. I felt a distant rage somewhere in me, but not the fire that had been there months prior. Exhaustion did things to a woman, and maybe in this case, it led to restraint and hilariously better tactical decisions. "You wouldn't even *exist* without me!" Undead survived at the cost of their minds slowly fracturing down to the core obsession that kept them with a tangible form; it was part of why there was no point in reasoning with Asuza: he legitimately didn't have the capability now, and that was assuming he ever had it to begin with, another thing I wasn't certain of. I didn't think it would affect bound undead incarnations like Kisate though because her mind was tied to a living body and she hadn't actually *lived* the whole time since her death; her mind effectively shut down between death and the next incarnation cycle, easily cutting out most of the time. I began to question my understanding of that theory with how much she just wouldn't *leave me alone,* however.

"Kisate, seriously, calm your ass down." Leah ran over, stepping between me and Kisate.

I knew full well the rage in Kisate: the anger, the desire. The hilarious similarities between us, and that those similarities were the origin of our disputes. I knew the ironies and that Kisate wasn't worth my time.

And yet.

Yet.

I took a deep breath as I stood, meeting Kisate's eyes once more. At the not-quite reflection. At the fact that Kylie — that I — *wasn't* a perfect reflection.

"You're right." Leah's head sharply turned at my words; surprise replaced her normally aloof features, ever so slightly widened eyes, lips faintly parted.

Kisate took the statement as a victory, huffing as she said, "I'm glad you *finally* understand your place."

The corners of my lips pulled into a grim smirk, eyes not leaving the woman that had essentially become prey. "I wasn't finished."

Leah said, "Oh fuck's sake, why's it so damn loud tonight?"

Kisate's eyes trained to a glare as she made a hand gesture to continue.

"I know." I turned my gaze to Chloé. "Hey Chloé, isn't it strange? How you and Kisate and Leah all have the same eye color, but Kylie and I don't?"

Kisate's eyes widened while Leah furrowed her brow. Chloé tilted her head once more. "Actually, now that you mention it, that *is* weird. Why is Kylie — Sia — different, Kisate? If it was just Sia, maybe, but Kylie's the same too. Did something go wrong with the spell? Was it...? Did I...?"

"Well?" I tilted my head much the same as Chloé had. But it wasn't a question of childish innocence as Chloé's had been: I didn't ask questions I didn't know the answer to. Not to enemies, and Kisate certainly wasn't my friend. "Why is that, Kisate?"

"You bitch," Kisate said. That was going on my trophy wall: an accomplishment worthy of the highest honors since it meant I'd thoroughly pissed her off.

Leah's head turned back to Kisate. "Kisate?"

"Maybe I can help a bit," I said. "*Sometime* between Chloé's birth and Kylie's birth, there was an alteration in the actual soul composition. It didn't affect Chloé because she was already born. It only took place once the next cycle started, because Kisate had already started planning for that, hadn't you?"

Kisate stepped back.

It wasn't enough. The pain she felt from this — the terror... it was nothing. Nothing compared to what I had felt. To what Kylie would feel.

"It just..."

I balled my fist. "It wasn't Asuza that killed Chloé. It was you. You're the one who used blood magic when she was on the edge. And you'd collaborated with Takite over it even, so he knew to follow through on his side when things happened." Chloé froze her movements, eyes moved down to the black nothingness of a subcon floor. "You took away yet another choice from myself in a life where I already got *jack shit* all choice. You were willing to kill one incarnation and permanently alter the core composition of another to get a weapon, so will you just sit down and shut the hell up? What was even the point of going that far if you're just going to micromanage and pretend like your twice failed plan is going to be better the third? Or are you saying you planned all along for Chloé to die and her living would've been a miscalculation? That Kylie living will be a miscalculation?"

Not even Leah spoke up in Kisate's defense this time, her eyes on Chloé. Chloé said nothing. Didn't know she had been defending her effective killer all this time, that maybe she'd have lived if Kisate hadn't used that last bit of mana, that maybe Dmitri *would've* made it in time if Kisate hadn't snuck around with blood magic at the end.

"I'm just..." Kisate had a whimper to her normally proud voice. Her lips quivered. "Do you know how much it hurts — to die, again and again?" A sharp inhale echoed through her chest. "Feeling it, over and over, and then having to take back seat until Activation, and never getting my own life. I can't do it again, I can't. I won't."

Leaning onto my hip, I placed my hand on said hip. "Then you need to back the hell off. This is *my* show, and I *will* win, whether it's against Asuza or *you,* by whatever means I deem necessary. Your time is over."

# Chapter Thirty-One
## good enough

The familiar door creak held a timidness as it slid open. Felt weird to say I remembered it like yesterday and remembered every more confident iteration after as well. Another joy of hypermnesia. *"That's Kylie. You care if I go ahead?"*

"The hell can you even tell?" Jordan asked.

*"Door sounds. Kyle doesn't open the door that slowly; she's too familiar with it. That slow's a Kylie thing."*

Jordan shook his head. "Fine." He should've added a bit more sulk to that pout, might've watered a plant.

Kylie stepped close, eyes glancing at me as I gained control over Jordan's body. Her eyes squinted b'fore she shook her head. "You're all so loud..."

An unfortunate fact I couldn't change if I tried. "Sorry."

*"'Loud'? Wait, fuck, she still? Even if you're the one...?"*

"Yeah? Just figured that out?" I said.

*"There's no damn benefit, fuck's sake."*

I could've argued 'bout that: being able to nap whenever without finding a spot to physically sleep'd been an unexpected perk, and free time to talk to those I couldn't've otherwise physically seen's up there pretty high too. Wasn't worth the argument though; he could have his bitch-fit in the corner while I got actual shit done.

Kylie's lips parted for a moment b'fore nodding. "It's um. It's Rota, right?"

This was the first time we'd directly interacted since Jordan's Act. That's something I hadn't really considered, but suddenly made things awkward as hell. I nodded, "Good enough at least."

"I, um. I've only really worked with Dani on more... physical stuff. And I'm apparently really bad at it."

Dani's a shitty teacher; I'd heard *those* stories enough times to inform me I'd made out missing those lessons.

"We all start somewhere." Once I practiced with Kylie for around an hour, our positions would swap: Kyle with Jordan, me and Kylie "in reserve." Was unfortunately the best way to work with an experienced partner actually able to spot right then. Who knew how many rounds we'd go through; depended on how long the younger two held up since hell knew Kyle'd dragged me to hell and back in our own training. "You know how to summon Isare, right?"

A light blush filled her cheeks. Wow. Wouldn't've thought she'd been able to sneak that one by Kyle. "Sorr — I am *not*, what you've all been silent all morning and *now* start?"

Having been on Kylie's side of this argument many times myself, I could only snicker. "Did Kyle tell you the full incantation?"

Another few seconds passed in silence, Kylie giving a brief nod while mouthing a few of the words. Prob'bly's trying to remember the spell, at least as a short term "get Kyle off her ass" measure. Her eyes briefly met mine b'fore lowering, as if she remembered *Jordan* wasn't there.

The distance stung more than I liked; I understood: I wasn't *her Jordan*. Just like she wasn't Kyle — *my Kylie*. That timidness and caution and awkwardness hurt like fuck, nonetheless.

She nodded, stepping back from me a foot or so b'fore taking a deep breath and releasing it. Kyle must've been instructing her, so I stayed quiet.

My memory made these moments so strange: if I didn't ponder, it's just a sense of déjà vu. If I ever stopped to recollect from when I was this-Jordan, though... I knew what was gonna happen next, like I was the one with precognition and not Kyle. The only exceptions're moments *Jordan* wasn't present, moments I wished for 'cause the déjà vu's creepy as fuck.

There's a shit-ton of things I wanted to change. Those moments were far away right then, though; instead, I saw an adorably inexperienced young woman in front of me, reaching her left hand out to air. My fingertips burned in anticipation of the incoming healing spell: this time ain't 'cause of my memory, but 'cause Isare's gonna fuck her wrist with that type of grip, and Kyle's a trial by fire instructor as ever.

"Isare," she said, as if testing the word on her lips. No confidence, but no terror either. More hesitance came from the rest of the spell: "H-heed your, um...mistress's call. Summon forth." Kylie winced as Isare materialized into her left hand; the weight's more than she expected. The staff clanked onto the concrete. "Ow... warning would've been nice!" Did she forget I was here? That shouldn't've been amusing, but it's so unlike the Kyle I was used to, always hyper-aware, always guarded.

"Here, gimme your hand," I said.

She nodded, a shy awkwardness as she held out her dominant hand. Laying my right hand on top of her left one, my aura manifested.

*"The fuck? That's... that's what Siani..."* Jordan hadn't gotten the memo that healing magic ain't restricted to Kyle. Dumbass, why would it be? *"Why ain't you do anything impressive like that b'fore?"*

"No need," I said to Jordan, removing my hand from on top of her wrist. "Should be better?"

She rotated her wrist before nodding. "Thank you."

"You ready to start again?"

Kneeling, she clutched Isare by the middle with both hands and then stood with the staff horizontally against her. "I think so. I don't... really know what to do. Kind of obvious since I hurt myself before we even started, I guess."

I most definitely ain't a staff user either — 'specially not one with retractable blades; I just'd trained with Kyle so long that I could get Kylie started on the basics, same as Kyle could with swordplay for Jordan. Fuck knew she didn't know how to use a sword, and it needed to stay that way with how painful fuckin' Isare's blades were as it was.

"S'alright, that's why we're here." I moved behind her, shifting her arms. "Starting out, we're not gonna work with the blades." The blades'd get me decapitated, and that'd put a damper on my whole living thing. She needed experience with just feeling the weight, how motions felt. To get bumped on the head a few times. Or well. Prob'bly few thousand, but still.

I pressed her shoulders down from where she'd tensed them at my touch.

"S-sorry." Damn, Dani had her so skittish. "I should've... I'm just not... very good."

Kyle'd have my ass later, but what Kylie needed right then ain't learning how to give someone a concussion; she needed someone to listen to her. The sessions with Dani'd gotten under her skin far more than I'd realized years ago when I was Jordan seeing this.

"Let's take a breather for a few. Just summoning Isare's a step, ten minute break."

"She, um, Sia that is, said — "

I snickered despite my best efforts. "Veto'ed, not happening, Kyle." Walking to one of the only-mildly shattered windows in this very technically defined building of a house, I sat on the concrete and patted beside me. Kylie hesitated b'fore she timidly nodded and walked over. She then pulled her knees to her chest, arms around her knees.

Called it.

"I'll try to practice more later. I should..."

Leaning against the wall, I glanced away; felt the cool concrete against the otherwise hot as fuck heat-trap of this house. The fact that this hadn't flagged more of my attention years ago's a problem. Was just another indication that my younger self's a dumb, self-absorbed jackass. "You can't learn everything she knows in one day." Not for a lack of trying, I knew damn sure. "You're gonna take things at your pace, and your pace's good enough."

I heard her shuffle but didn't look over to see how she'd repositioned. "I just... If Dani's not good enough, how am I supposed to be better than that? She's been in karate since she was basically in diapers. If... if... things happen, then... if she was useless then..."

"That's why it's not just you here right now." I wanted to hold her, stroke her hair, tell her that things'd be okay. That she'd be okay. That things'd get better.

But it ignored that things'd get worse b'fore better. It ignored that I knew there're some things I couldn't say.

"I don't... I don't want anyone else to die because of..."

An ethical dilemma I'd never shared: as Jordan, was too self-absorbed, and now...

My hands were far from clean.

"What's happened with Dani? Sounds like trouble?"

Out of the corner of my eye, I saw her run hands through her scalp as a sigh came from her. "Yeah... it's the first time we've ever fought like that... first time I've ever been seeing her this... just... mean." Territorial, she meant. "Jordan" impeded on Dani's *territory* of "Kylie's protector."

I wanted to bang my head into a goddamn wall from how idiotic both my younger self and Dani were, how it was 'bout *them*, not their friend whose life was in danger, who had to sleep with one eye open. "Give it some time. Pro'bly feels like lifetimes, but it's not even been half a year. Still a lot changing for both of you."

Her eyes turned to me, so I turned to give her more direct attention. Her lips pushed together, eyes glazed over; those were the typical tells she focused in on empathic reads, so must've been focusing on my emotions for some reason. "It's weird."

"Hm?"

"You're different than Sia." I bit back "no shit" 'cause there's only one Kyle; world couldn't support that much chaos and hellfire. She bit her bottom lip. "It's like... you're like Jordan, but... not. Something's so... different." I could only chuckle: maturity's a hell'va thing. "Could I ask you something?"

I nodded. Didn't like that tone one bit, 'specially while she's so clearly reading the shit outta me. Well, me and the other souls in this body, but still. I knew the question though, remembered it from when I'd been *Jordan*, and I knew I was the best one to answer it. "Sure, 'sup?"

Her attention fully turned toward me, eyes less glazed over.

**165**

"I, um, I know Sia's mentioned him, but you seem to know more about that guy, the one that's..." Her left hand gripped her absorption device as her head lowered, eyes focusing on a crack in the concrete. "Why me?"

Kyle knew jack shit 'bout the politics that'd gone on in Riyati. Never cared. Never would besides when it'd affect her. I moved my gaze back to the other side of the training house. "Asuza Nuueti. He was Kisate's direct servant. The Nuueti's're one of the potential backup lines for succession mates. Was a couple years younger than her, but never liked Takite, who Kisate was engaged to. Wasn't helped by the general Nuueti family hating that the crown'd picked the Tanoti line — Takite's family line — over them that round. Went to whoever had the highest estimated max magipoten, and Takite won the bid basically." I was waiting for Takite to call me out on details 'bout his life that I knew so well when he wasn't sure how I knew anything at all. Was funny that despite having no empathic abilities, I could almost feel him shifting uncomfortably.

"So Takite, that's like, to you and Jordan, Kisate is for, um...?"

It's cute how she couldn't say "original incarnation," so fought against acknowledging it. Kyle's basically the same still. Maybe I would've been too if I didn't have hypermnesia. "Yeah. He and Kisate're the two that're intended for the reincarnation spell, for the ruling line's survival."

I heard her shuffle once more; turning, I saw she'd moved her head on top of her knees, propped up by her chin. "Survival of what? They died right after, right? Kisate's like around Sia's age, so... How'd that help anything survive?" This's a story I knew well, had read 'bout, had seen glimpses of. Yet, I didn't wanna say it, not right then, not when people who died from it're *right there*. Felt insensitive. "Rota?"

Balling my right fist into a light grip, I lowered my head. "Sorry, Takite, Kisate." I also knew Kylie had a right to know.

While I'd prob'ly never know if Kisate said anything, Takite said, *"It's understandable, for her to ask. If you know, it's all right."*

His words made sense in a way they hadn't when I'd been on Jordan's side of this. It was shit I shouldn't've known, not now. Should've been lost to time. Was a question that Leah nor

Chloé nor Dmitri nor John'd ever thought to really ask, hadn't had the time. I nodded. "Only reason the Nuueti family accepted the 'disgrace' of Asuza being first servant to Kaku Kiseti — Kisate's formal title — is 'cause they wanted to stage a coup and use Asuza to get info for them. He'd always been creepy as fuck and didn't understand the damn meaning of 'consent,' but he did fall for Kisate in whatever fucked up definition his brain has of it."

*"Wait, you're defendin' the jackass that's tried to get people to kidnap her?"* Jordan said, suddenly jumping into the conversation. I ignored him; of course, I ain't defending that bastard. But history ain't written in black and white, and it's all part of the context for how now came to be.

"Asuza's family didn't much care for him not killing Kisate in her sleep and shit like that. Kinda put a damper on their treason schemes. So they went around him, and he found out last minute, tried to warn Kisate." I watched as Kylie tensed, fingers gripping her knees. I wondered what was said then that I couldn't hear — was it Kyle or Kisate herself adding to the story? Thinking on it, Kisate and Takite knew what'd happened until their deaths from the reincarnation spell, but I prob'ly knew better past then — they'd never seen the post-death records and accounts and shit. My voice softened. "Dunno why Kisate believed him — she'd answer that better. But only reason she and Takite're here now's 'cause she did, and the head general cast the reincarnation spell as the incited coupe were trying to beat down the door for where they'd hid. Asuza gave enough time for a backup plan to assure the line carried down, since there was a full riot of shit-stirrers that'd basically overrun the castle."

Kylie's voice was soft as she asked, "But then why? If he wanted Kisate to be safe, why's he...? And why'd he, to Leah and Chloé?"

Asuza didn't love Kisate. Never had. Infatuation maybe, but he'd never loved her. Never truly knew her, even. Couldn't've listed her bad traits and stuck around regardless, only saw this idealized princess, paragon of perfection. It'd be like saying Kyle's warm and strong and brilliant without the admission she's an outright bitch when she wanted to be, stubborn as a damn rock wall 'bout the most *inane* goddamn shit sometimes, and getting her to be honest's a fuckin' hellride.

"He never tried to actually understand her. Still ain't."

Kylie tilted her head to observe me as she continued resting her head on her knees. "But why would you kill someone you like? That's just dumb at that point."

She was still so naïve. Kinda surprised Kyle ain't having her ass for that line of thinking, but... guess we both knew it wouldn't last; there wasn't a point to chiding her when we knew she'd learn far better than myself even. "He won't understand her. Thinks that Takite and every incarnation since's forced on her, and that he knows what's best for her over everyone else."

Her lips pursed together into a thin line. "I don't even like anyone though — Jordan's just my *friend*, and I..." I wondered if she even realized she's lying through her damn teeth there? Prob'ly not. She'd always been great at not seeing things she didn't like. "Can't I just explain — and wait, how's someone from that long ago still around anyways? He's not like Kisate and Takite where he's in someone else's head, right?"

I shook my head. "You're better off asking Kyle to explain the theory on exactly how that works. But basically, with enough willpower and magipoten, technically people can live past their death — records indicate his parents killed him when they found out he'd given Kisate warning. That whole shit show's recorded as 'The Fall of Riyati,' 'cause even if the crown had problems, ain't nothing compared to how inept the Nuueti's were at running shit. Ran the crown into the ground in less than two years, had no heir 'cause they killed him, and well. Yeah. Riyati vanished from history basically."

Takite's voice was soft as he said, *"So that's what happened."* It was as I'd expected, then: I knew more than themselves 'bout what'd happened after their deaths. They'd never found out. And given that Kylie looked even more distracted, I imagined Kisate had words of her own right then.

"Right then," I said as I stood. I offered her my hand but knew she wouldn't take it. "Let's switch off. Time for the other two to do some shit while we catch a break."

# Chapter Thirty-Two
## mirror reflection

Jordan | June 22
Boyle Residence

When would this shitty week end?

My arms ached from yesterday's training: the Siani that'd healed my injuries's a different Siani than the one who pushed and pushed and wouldn't stop fuckin' pushing me yesterday. Part of me'd found it kinda hot to be that close to her, her breath in my ear, guiding my arms. That disappeared to the far reaches of hell not half an hour later when she had me keep swinging that damn sword. Keep doing the one swipe, stance, whatever the hell she'd called it.

Whole fuckin' thing's a damn mistake anyways.

*"Mhmm. So if you mix the milk in at —"* Rotanu just *had* to have a conversation with Dmitri right then. Couldn't they've waited 'til I was asleep? Yet again, I couldn't tune them out. Had the lights off in my room. Had always shared a bedroom, and it was weird it's only with Thomas at the moment; he's already asleep despite the cheap blinds barely keeping the sun out. Also fuck the sun not setting 'til like 9pm in the summer.

I pulled the patched blanket over my head, muttering a hushed, "Trying to damn sleep here."

*"Then try harder. No one's stopping you."*

Tightening my eyes, I wished my lower spine didn't ache.

I wanted to pretend the worst's from Siani. It ain't. She'd been harsh, strict, but there's an element of softness, tenderness. She didn't hurt me, just pushed me to be more than I was meant to be. Shouted no names at me, never hit or kicked.

Nothing like this afternoon'd been.

Rolling over on my side, I used my left hand to hold the blanket as high up as my arm would reach. I moved my right hand in the space between, hovering in the air. Focusing as Takite'd taught me, a small flame — like something from a lighter — hovered above my palm. There was warmth, but it didn't hurt. Not like it should've, having the hottest part of the flame not even a third of an inch from my skin. Closing my fingers around the flame, there was no pain. Just warmth. Opening my fingers once more, I dismissed the flame.

It's terrifying. Inhuman. If my father knew, he would've had even more names for me.

Everything's too damn complicated.

Lowering my left arm, I tightened my eyes. Wished things didn't hurt. Wished I wasn't able to recall the afternoon with precise clarity, over and over.

I no longer felt the blanket on me. Or my mattress. Black all around me.

Other men were there, somehow illuminated, yet no light source. The youngest of them looked around my age, sitting cross-legged and watching one of the older ones standing that was speaking —

A voice I knew well, thanks to my new memory.

The speaking man had olive brown hair tied back in a low ponytail, front strands too short to be held in the ponytail. Had the same light blue eyes as myself — a difference between the other men, who all had a darker blue hue in comparison. The man had on jeans, tennis shoes, and a button-down shirt and a light jacket on.

I knew who this was, but there's no way this man's my future: with what money to dress that nice? I'd been wearing most of my clothes for years, what didn't fit me anymore went to Thomas. Never anything new. Never anything nice. I'd never have luxuries like that.

Matching light blue eyes met mine; Kylie'd called my eye color ice-blue years ago when we'd been looking at color names for some project, and the description's now morbidly hilarious. "Oh, wanted to join in? Just had'ta ask."

Breaking eye contact, I wanted to look at the floor, but there was none. Just like all the surrounding's around us, black with more black. "Don't even know where this is. Or why I'm here."

"Don't you?" Rotanu asked.

I very obviously didn't 'cause I wouldn't have literally just said otherwise. "No?"

"This is where you go when Rota takes control," another man said — was around Rotanu's age, so it had to have been John or Takite. The younger one that'd been sitting and listening to Rotanu must've been Dmitri. Each their own people. Only Rotanu matched me perfectly outside of age, but all of them're like looking in a mirror's reflection, the darker blue eye color as the only difference.

I'd never focused on anything but staying connected with my body when Rotanu took control. But I knew this place, could remember it when referencing the times he had control.

This ain't right. Nothing 'bout this's right. Wasn't how things're meant to be.

Yet why did everything line up?

# Chapter Thirty-Three

## dynamic changes

Siani | June 23
Rae Residence

I had always been a rip the band-aid off type of person, even if it was thirty of them at once, and I just couldn't do that this time, needed to be patient, time things *perfectly*.

"Sia..." There was a whine in Kylie's tone. She didn't want a "cram session," as she had irritably described what I made her do right then.

It wasn't exactly wrong.

*"Mm?"* I asked; I knew what Kylie was about to say but gave the opening anyway.

"Most teen girls are going out on, I don't know. Sleepovers? Dates? Not being shoved in front of a notebook for what's effectively become an entire school subject."

*"Oh, didn't know you had someone you're interested in — who's the lucky guy?"* Chuckling, I added, *"Or girl, whichever works."*

I knew the answer, of course. And I knew which answer Kylie would give: "Wh... that's not what I meant. Just like, I don't want to be doing this."

*"And I want to hear about this date idea. Fascinating, do tell more."*

Things so obvious now were murky at best back then. Nothing in me wanted to go back to these years. And I technically wasn't — had my memories that had changed me, wasn't this Kylie whining and not even to the blushing stage.

Kylie let out an aggravated huff. "Where's Leah? Or Chloé? Even Kisate's been quiet lately."

I wasn't sure if I was over-suppressing some of Kylie's empathic abilities accidentally or if she was truly just that dense. I desperately wanted it to be the former, but was fairly certain that the adjustment ratios were still correct: Kylie's magipoten was growing faster than her own adaptation of empathy, so I was constantly adjusting the ratios of control and suppression; it was unsurprising since we had barely broken the ice in working through that beast and instead had focused on other core concepts, but it also meant I was constantly shouldering my own empathy — not to mention the sensory precognition — and additional readings from Kylie due to not wanting to completely block out empathy: it was something Kylie *had* to learn to live with; it wasn't going away, and even the smallest progress in adapting to it on the back-burner was *something*.

*"Not here to save you, as you can see. Now get back to it: what are the branches of foundational magic? On the paper, get going."* Kylie grumbled but picked her pencil back up. She wrote down mostly correct information, but still missed a few things. Here we went again... *"Second line wrong. That's not even a word."*

Leaning back in her chair, Kylie set the pencil down. "I can't believe I'm saying this, but I actually wish I was just back in school at this point: at least I get grades."

*"Oh, you want a letter? C, passing, except for the part where if you used a scanning spell and tried to infuse elemental aspects, you'd probably shoot out your vision from air pressure."*

"Shouldn't like, Jordan be here for this? Why's he get to skip?"

Because I spent enough years of my life dragging Rota through forced study as it was, and the best fight Kylie could put up was nothing compared to the punting I regularly did to get him to open a damn book he'd have memorized in thirty seconds anyway.

I was completely not giving that answer, though. Besides, Rota was the one responsible for whatever Jordan did (and more likely, *didn't*) learn; it was enough of a pain getting Kylie and Jordan physically together as it was.

*"Need I remind you, based off past patterns,* he *isn't the one whose very life depends on getting this right.* You *are."*

I felt Kylie tense, hand going to her absorption device for comfort. Felt the helplessness invade through Kylie and then my own being, the knot in my stomach despite not having a physical body at the moment. "Can we just... not talk about that? Please?"

So much so, I wished I could comply, could just hug Kylie and tell her it would be okay.

But I couldn't.

*"Let's switch to theory."*

Kylie nodded; I took control of her body and then turned to a new a page of the notebook, writing concepts long since seared into my brain. "Magipoten chart ranges work off percentage of magic within body composition, as we've discussed prior."

*"Mm."*

It was no secret Kylie wasn't paying attention right then. That was fine enough for a moment, though; at least she would have the notes to reference back on when she needed to review over it. And she would. Many times.

"Body changes formally start post-Act."

*"Mm."*

"But while there's some *stasis* changes — like symbols, as previously discussed — , there's some dynamic ones too." I picked the pencil up in my left hand, writing out an outline as I spoke. "Two ones I want to cover before we break." As expected, those words would've caused Kylie's ears to perk up if she was in control of her body.

If only there was more time, but realistically, there would never be enough time. Every day had to count because I needed to teach her how to fly while there still was a nest.

*"Only two?"* she asked, suddenly interested for completely non-altruistic reasons.

"For now." I wrote out "Wings" on the page; I felt a recoil from Kisate, who had snuck in sometime. She said nothing, however. Likely another thing I wasn't "supposed" to know about but was in fact rather familiar with.

*"'Wings'? Is that an acronym?"*

175

"Nope."

*"Wait, so if this is body changes then I'll... you can't be serious."*

"First off: there's a reason I said these fall under *dynamic*. They're not applicable all the time. Second, very few individuals can utilize wings." Writing "85+" under the Wings heading, I said, "The typical max magipoten threshold — so where an individual would cap out at magipoten — is around 85."

*"So if you're too high, then it doesn't work? I'm confused why we're even covering it then because I thought you said it's important —"*

"Wrong way of looking at max. And admittedly, not the metric I probably should've started with, thinking on it." That got me a bit of an internal glare, but I deserved it; I wasn't a professional teacher, and everyone seemed to forget that when I had to teach something. "The break threshold is around 65. The reason max is typically used is because that can flux a bit, whereas max says if it's even worth looking at. As a reminder, my — *your* — max is 90. Above 85. So guess what?"

*"Jordan's at least stuck with this too, right?"*

Kylie's attempt to be stealthy utterly failed: she just didn't want to be alone, and I wasn't sure who she wanted to fool otherwise. "Mm. Jordan's max is 86, right at the evaluation point. While neither of you have utilized a spell that would trigger them yet, when you start working more intensively with Rota and my form respectively, you'll have access to wings." I glanced back down at the page. "They're what could be considered 'magic exhaust' in a way. When you summon past a certain threshold of magic at once, they materialize. And as weird as they sound now, they were actually a really high-status thing in Riyati since only high nobility could manifest them." It felt weird to mention Riyati while Kisate said nothing.

Leah and Chloé's faith in Kisate had shattered, leaving the atmosphere *amazing* for all of us all except Kylie, who had missed the entire event and had yet to pick up on anything. I wasn't sure if this frigidness was what I wanted; while I didn't want to fight Kisate every moment, still had a fury for what Kisate had caused, but...

I understood. That was probably the worst part, even.

*"Do they like... just go away when the spell finishes then?"*

"Not quite. Like spells need mana gathered and channeled, that same concept goes into dismissing wings. It's not necessarily *hard*. It's just they're really sensitive and keep you in a high magic consumption state, so it's not ideal unless you're doing something specific that would require that level of mana gathered."

*That* got Kisate's attention as she finally said, "You've *summoned wings?*"

*"Oh, Kisate, morning — or um, afternoon, I guess."*

I bit back a snicker at how forced Kylie's attempt at the greeting was. "Many times, to answer your question. As has Rota."

*"How? You're both still so young... Sorry. Carry on."*

Kisate was only like a year or two older than Rota and me. Rota had read that it typically took decades to learn how to use wings, which was likely what Kisate referred to. I wasn't sure if Kisate ever had used them or even seen them on another for that matter.

Yet another fun difference between war and peace: enough life and death situations really sped up the learning process if your survival to the next day depended on mastering the concept.

"So that's wings. Not going to work with them today, just introducing the concept." The pencil point hovered just above the page. I didn't want to write this next part.

It needed to be said.

But like so many things lately, I didn't want to be the one to say it.

*"Sia?"*

"Sorry, was distracted." I pushed the pencil point to the page, writing out "Berserk state." "This is divided as well, but I'm just covering one part of it right now since it's the part that cleanly falls under the dynamic subcategory." Another hesitation, though I recovered quick enough that Kylie didn't notice. "We've talked about absorption devices before. This is the 'what if' that happens if contact is lost long enough that surplus build up happens more than the mental and physical load can tolerate."

*"Those are... words. I think."*

I laughed. A valid attempt to understand jargon that would

one day become so natural. "So, when an absorption device loses contact with the host, the stored magic starts cycling back to the host rapidly. But while that's going on, keep in mind the absorption device was there to prevent going past the host's limits — physical and mental — because the body tends to generate more magic than it can handle. That excess needs to offload. So the host will be slammed with too much mana, and that'll cause what's called 'berserk' or 'berserk state.' Physical alterations include..." I wrote "physical" and below it as a bulleted list, "eye changes," "hair changes." "Eyes gain... it's like a wild energy, something you'll know when you see it, trust me. Is in the iris, usually both eyes are equally affected but not always. Doesn't really do anything to vision one way or another. Hair is more of a mess, especially if prolonged: starting at the roots and down the strand, hair color changes to reflect the mage's aura. Can eventually be all your hair, and post that, starts growing hair out rapidly."

*"Like permanent hair dye?"*

"Not permanent, unless hair actively grows out, then that part is. But the color from already grown hair fades in time once no longer berserked." Filling my — well, Kylie's — lungs with air, I wrote "mental" and then "loss of consciousness; feral instinct emergence."

*"That looks... far less promising. Maybe I want to go back to the hair dye Mom'd ground me for life over."*

Cracking my neck, I nodded. "You do. But here we are." Setting the pencil down, I stared at the page. "It's hard to explain, to be honest. It's like your mind fades out, and base instincts take over: safety, food, shelter..."

I couldn't use the phrase I wanted: "feral animal." Didn't want Kylie to have that association any sooner than she would.

*"How long's that for? Just a few minutes? Or like...?"*

"Until the over-supply is rectified and the absorption device can absorb back down to tolerable thresholds."

*"Oh."*

And that might've been the most accurate reaction possible.

# Chapter Thirty-Four

## the first test

Rotanu | June 25
Opal Pines Park

I wasn't sure how I could feel goddamn sick as fuck without a body. Damn subcon could've lacked that replication of my anxiety, but of course not. That would've been too simple.

Jordan and Kylie sat on the usual bench at the park, were talking 'bout something I couldn't focus on if I tried. Kylie'd noticed something's off, but my emotions blurred with Jordan's and Takite's and John's and Dmitri's. Saved my ass, truth be told.

"Ain't matter, just ignore 'em," Jordan said.

"I guess." Kylie was not remotely assured. I didn't blame her. Her eyes glanced away a moment b'fore redirecting to Jordan. "He knows what it means?" Another pause. "Sure, I guess. Um... Sia asked for me to tell you, Rota, that she knows."

*Kylie* might not have figured out that I was the apprehensive one, but *Kyle's* most certainly skilled enough to do so. It must've given her confirmation without me saying a word.

The first test: the first time I truly had to trust, and fuck, I was not a fan of this. I'd rather be oblivious than know, 'specially since I was notoriously shit at concealing my own emotions. Was kind of ironic actually, considering I'm engaged to an empath.

"Huh, knows what?" Jordan asked.

Kylie shook her head. "Didn't say, said it was just something between the two of them, but that Rota'd get it."

Jordan leaned back as he scoffed. "Doubt it. He's such a damn ditz, Takite's constantly having to cover for 'em as it is."

If Jordan's half as smart as he thought, something would've flagged that I said nothing to defend myself. Of course he didn't notice, too stuck up his own ass.

I mentally took a deep breath and released it. That ain't fair to him; I was just anxious as all fuckin' hell, and Jordan's an exceptionally easy target to misplace that energy onto. However, Jordan's also kinda asking to be snapped at. Looking back, I was a little shit when I was younger, and I hadn't realized the full extent 'til right then when I was dealing with it as an adult.

"'Cover'?" Kylie asked. "How so? You... you don't have anything like empathy right?"

Jordan paused; he was having an internal bitch-fit over Kylie acknowledging the objective truth that he's a mage and changes'd come with it. He shook his head after a few seconds. "Nah, nothing like that. Just some shit with my memory. And the dumbass ain't even able to help despite nothing on the level Siani's dealing with from what they've said."

*Rota?* John asked. Made sense he's the one who caught on first, being the one trained in watching people. Dmitri'd just been a shopkeep's son and Takite's effective royalty — was pledged to the eldest child of the ruling line, had been brought up as a king-in-training but not in the matters of everyday civil life, of watching his back else it be sliced open.

*Hm?* I knew John's next question, but Kyle'd give me hell if I let anything on. I had to trust her. Believe in her. No matter if it hurt like fuck.

*You've been rather quiet the whole day. Is something wrong?*

*Eh, tired. Ain't sleep right last night.*

*I see.* John didn't believe me. Unsurprising, to say the least.

"Thanks," Kylie said. "For today. I just... have had a lot on my mind lately, with... everything. Just having someone else that understands..." Her eyes were wide, open, *innocent*. An expression I wished Kyle would have. Sometimes still did, despite everything.

Jordan moved his eyes away from Kylie, rather annoyingly cutting off my view of her. I wanted to keep watching so I could read her body language. Unfortunately, that's the downside of not having my own body: I didn't get to call shots on such things as where my attention focused, and unlike Kyle, I'd never learned how to read auras. Actually, it's prob'bly better said that she was *why* I had never learned how to read auras: why bother when she's so proficient in it?

"Y-yeah. I mean, I ain't got half the shit you got." Bullshit, at least in the way Jordan said it. Kylie just said how thankful she was to have someone with her, and my younger self's best response was to blow her off to spare his ego.

And the other three wondered *why* I was a smartass to Jordan; it was better than cussin' his ass out like I wanted to right then.

"I guess you're right," she said, her voice softer.

She wasn't *my Kyle*. But hearing that soft tone — hurt, vulnerable, rejected — stung like the words'd been said to me. I didn't love her like she was my fiancée, didn't feel the adoration I felt for my partner. She's too young, too inexperienced, not the woman I had slept with, bled with.

But it didn't stop me from wanting to prevent the pain she so obviously felt right then. At how alone she sounded, even without me seeing her actual expression. At how I wanted to hug her and tell her she wasn't alone, Jordan's just an immature jackass.

"What time's it?" Jordan asked.

"Um, looks like just past four."

"Shit," he said. I took a deep breath; Jordan moved his expression back to Kylie. "I gotta get home. Supposed to fix dinner tonight."

"Oh, right, sorry. I'll see you tomorrow then for more *fun* with Sia and Rota."

Jordan cursed again under his breath. "Worse than damn class at this rate. But yeah, see you then." I watched her stay seated as Jordan turned and walked away.

I took another deep breath.

# Chapter Thirty-Five

## berserk

I watched Jordan walk off; I made sure he faded from sight before rubbing my eyes, feeling them water.

He was right: as much as he was tied to the same new and foreign rules for our bodies and minds and whatever being a *mage* entailed that I learned daily, we weren't the same.

No one wanted him dead.

Mom wouldn't be home for another few hours, and while crying alone on a park bench must have looked strange, my legs just wouldn't move. I needed a few moments to myself, or at least as "to myself" as I could get right then. Sniffling, I lowered my arm. Was I ready?

Nope, another set of tears fell. Moving my arm up, I felt something forcing my arm inward, constricting, beady. I forced my arm outward, that constricted feeling disappearing.

Tensing, I felt emotions flood me, consume me.

*"Wait, how?!"* Kisate was panicked. Almost terrified. *"Didn't you reinforce the spell?"*

*"Hm?"* Sia was distracted. *"Did, yeah."*

*"Then how — "*

So loud.

I winced, opening my eyes and seeing outlines extend far beyond what my normal eyesight could see somehow. Like the day Sia had been unconscious. Auras, Leah had called them.

"Why...?" Empathic readings increased by the moment. My brain felt like mush. No room for my own emotions, just a sea of terror and anxiety and despair.

*"Where is it?"* Kisate yelled. *"Find it!"*

"Find what...?"

Sia spoke, but her voice was strained. Maybe even the most strained I had heard it since that day there was a sensory precognition attack. *"Your absorption device's lost contact. I'm stalling out berserk on you, but it's... rough, and you're getting the empathy reads I normally filter plus some from the berserk. Forget the chain — go for the ring itself, you need contact. Like now."*

*"I don't care about the effects, a spike this large —"* Kisate's voice grew more distant. Faded, like yelling through a tunnel, echoing but indiscriminate.

A bright orange color came closer.

Leah's voice held terror as she said, *"Shit, shit, no..."*

I stood, felt myself sway; every movement seemed so sluggish, every breath suddenly measured. Kneeling, I saw this bright aquamarine and clouded-blue glow — was that it, the absorption device?

Sia winced; an intensity flashed through me, dropped me to my knees. My mind grew quieter, calmer. For the first time in weeks, I felt absolutely no fear.

Craving the warmth from my absorption device, I reached out; I felt a painful jolt as consciousness shot through me. My chest heaved; I saw a few aquamarine strands of hair pass by my cheek.

That had been the berserk that Sia had mentioned. I had almost lost all consciousness. "Sia?" I called.

No response.

*"She's out cold, but..."* Chloé sounded terrified; it was the first time I had ever heard her be anything but chipper; her voice mirrored mine of late.

That bright orange aura — a hunger — moved closer; I heard footsteps.

Who was about to see how much of a freak I looked like? Who was about to see me barely able to stand?

My hand shook as I pushed the ring onto my left index finger; my mind returned by the moment, but I still felt emotional and aura readings since Sia was unconscious. I saw the string that had snapped from my neck.

"I finally found you again." A male voice, eerily still in tone, came closer; he had to be the one that was so hungry, but not in a food way. It was deeper, darker, foreign. I turned around and saw a man who had empty green eyes, long blonde hair; his clothes were strange yet familiar, similar in style to what Kisate wore in the subcon.

Similar to Kisate...

"No..." I stepped backwards, falling onto the bench I had sat on with Jordan.

The man kneeled, kissing my right hand. "I've come to save you, Your Highness."

Then my world went black.

# Chapter Thirty-Six

## the first test

Jordan | June 25
Boyle Residence

I should've stayed longer. Would've if I knew this damn shitstorm waited for me.

One week. That was how long we had to pack up this time. My father hadn't bothered to even give us the full two-week notice he had; he sure as hell ain't helping pack us, already beat the shit outta me and then stormed out 'bout how no one understood how hard he worked.

I wasn't sure I'd ever seen my father hold down a job for over three months. Always bounced from minimum wage to minimum wage job just so he had something to submit on welfare checks. "Gainful employment," I had seen written on the documents.

This's why we never bothered unpacking. It's yet another inevitability. Yet another letdown. It's fine — this apartment sucked ass anyways. Maybe the next one would at least be closer to my high school.

Collecting more clothes, I shoved them in the black plastic trash bag. Once Thomas went to bed, I'd ask Rotanu or Takite to heal whatever'd gotten fucked earlier. Was the one good thing to come outta this, and I was fully intent on utilizing it.

Not that I wanted to learn how they did it because fuck that, it's a mistake I even knew 'bout any of this. But at least it'd cut down on the fuckin' throbbing headache I once again had.

*"Something up, Rota? You've been really quiet all day,"* Dmitri asked.

*"Ah, yeah, had some shit on my mind,"* he said.

If Rotanu *remembered* this was going to happen, a warning would've been a hell'va appreciated. I wouldn't have gone home right then. Let someone else be the punching bag for fuckin' once.

Actually, wait: I could confirm that my memory had exponentially sharpened since *that time*. Remembered and could recall like a movie with pausing and playing exact moments for anything that'd happened after *Act*, and this was *b'fore* my memory's as *robust* as Rotanu's implied his was.

Why the fuck'd Rotanu never once bothered to warn me?

"Why didn't you fuckin' tell me I was coming home to get my ass beat?" I whispered, trying to keep my voice low enough that Thomas didn't hear me.

*"Sorry, just been distracted."* Rotanu was not at all remorseful. He wasn't even damn pretending.

"And the other times?"

*"I gotta call it, I think."* Rotanu gave so few damns that he didn't even gimme a bullshit answer, just changed the damn subject. *"Super exhausted. Can you take point on auras tonight, Takite?"*

*"Oh, sure. Rest well."* Takite was prob'bly as surprised as the rest of us considering Rotanu never went to sleep b'fore me.

And more importantly: for being "myself from the future," Rotanu's a damn unreliable idiot that had absolutely no problem with making my life even further hell. At least the other three didn't know what's coming.

There's no way in fuckin' hell Rotanu's a future me: I wasn't a smartass, wasn't gonna fuck around and laugh and —

He's too damn familiar with Kylie, and it pissed me off. Made me even more pissed off that Siani's so familiar with him and that *softness* from her I noticed months ago's 'cause Siani connected me and Rotanu and that's *just wrong*. She's wrong. He's wrong. Yet again, this whole damn thing's wrong.

# Chapter Thirty-Seven

## no fear

Siani | June 26
Asuza's Castle

Everything hurt, and the best description of the pain was probably "hurt like hell." Wasn't the first time, wouldn't be the last time. Mana drain sucked, and berserk always sent the body into chaos before we even factored the current mana drain going on.

Opening my eyes, I saw torches illuminating the stone walls they were mounted on. I briefly wondered if Asuza bothered to relight the things or if he used a recast loop spell to keep them perma-lit. Also, how often was this room used, anyway? Was this the same place that Leah and Chloé died? I had no idea and doubted they'd be much for conversation once they woke up. Neither John nor Dmitri had made it before Asuza killed Leah and Chloé; the Kaku Tiza line only knew where Asuza showed the bodies, not where the actual murder kept happening. That's why Rota's memory was key in this, how we'd win, assuming Jordan's resolve solidified in time — even if Rota forced Jordan here right now, it wouldn't matter without Jordan's full cooperation, something that wouldn't be secured easily, not with the amount of self-doubt Jordan still had at this age.

Maybe I'd been in these situations too often when I no

longer felt panic from them. No fear. No concern at my wrists tied to the arms of a metal chair, rope rubbing against skin; though to be technical, it wasn't *my* body but Kylie's, and I'd just gained control since I was the first to wake up. There was an element of looseness in the rope. Could marginally flex my wrist still. A tighter rope pressed my fingers against and into each other before tying them down onto the metal chair arm. Ankles weren't much better, also tied down. Unfortunately, Kylie wore shorts and ankle socks: they made sense for late June's weather but were less ideal for rope rubbing against ankle skin. Another rope secured around my waist, further tying me to this metal chair, and more importantly, to the wires I felt strapped into my back; those wires ran to somewhere else in the room, filled with red — Kylie's blood. Thinking about it, literally draining the blood from someone was actually up there with miserable ways to murder them; there was an art to it I could appreciate despite it being squarely my problem at the moment.

My vision already held a faint blurriness; it made sense given we'd probably been out a solid ten hours, maybe more. Good news was the sleep and rapid overflow from loss of contact with the absorption device had bought more time: mana recharge was faster, which meant this body had more resources available to heal itself. Still had been a sizable net loss, though; this body had less than a day of fight left in it, and I wasn't sure my odds with even twelve hours now that one of us was awake: if even one consciousness was up, body recovery rates decreased. In the best case, we were going to be right down to the wire.

I licked my lower lip; it wasn't chapped because of the humidity in the air, so there was that.

Closing my eyes to concentrate, I allowed my consciousness to merge into the power around me; I wasn't sure if Kisate knew how to do so, but the rest certainly didn't. There were four auras within what I'd estimate was the building I was in — wasn't sure exactly what to call the place; wasn't a castle, but the architecture was too old for me to guess what it had once been. Just stone everywhere, bits of outside air tempting in. Was definitely milder in weather than Opal Pines had been, with hints of ocean salts still carried in the air. Though it wasn't all that to be more pleasant than June in Opal Pines.

This was hilarious in so many respects. The irony of it all. Definitely wasn't something I could've appreciated as *Kylie* back years ago.

Silence echoed in whatever this room could be called. No real outside light.

One of the auras — bright red — moved toward the room I was in. As the door creaked open, I opened my eyes. I couldn't see because of the darkness in the room, but the door sounded like it had a metal bottom, probably a wood composition that had been reinforced. Cheap.

Her outer irises were light green, tinting to a darker green further in her iris: signs of artificial magic transfer and life extension; it was fascinating he pulled that off actually, let alone at least three times. Dark brown hair was to her shoulders, slight curls. Probably around 5'8" or so, slim build. Slight makeup.

A glare I still remembered well: Nimaka.

"Oh, you're awake," she said. My empathy was stronger than Kylie's, but at least the increased pull wasn't placed directly on her body, instead pulling from my own in the future; my body was used to it, nothing new. Because I had my strength of empathy, however, it meant that I got full scope to the unbridled anger Nimaka hid behind a sweet tone. False security, cute. "Don't worry, it'll be all over soon," she said as she stepped closer and checked the wires, pushing one even further through my skin.

Speaking of opportunities I could only get once, this was one of them. "Even if I die, you'll still be nothing but a failed replacement that won't ever satisfy him."

That caught Nimaka's attention: no surprise, *Kylie* didn't know, not yet. None of them did, actually, except me and Rota. That veiled anger shifted to malice as she tightened the binding ropes on each arm, leg, and stomach, that looseness gone and tearing into skin. Fresh blood filled my senses as I felt thick liquid dripping down my hands, tips of my socks already clinging from that same liquid, a familiar iron smell. Nimaka then punched me across the cheek, dislodging my jaw momentarily. "You bitch."

Oh, that woke Kisate up. Unfortunately, I had other

problems to deal with over Nimaka now. Chief on that list was shutting Kisate up even though she hadn't said a word yet.

*"No... You failed."* Kisate's voice was calm, defeated almost. The expected anger filled Kisate a second later as her mind further woke up. *"After all that. After all those lectures, all those..."* Kisate clawed for control of Kylie's body; I gave it to her since I had gotten what I wanted as Nimaka stomped off, slamming the isolated room shut. Kisate tried to use telekinetics to snap the connected wires, but Kylie's body didn't have enough even at normal capacity to pull that off with the thickness of those attached wires; it was a waste of effort and mana. Maybe one or two could be destroyed, but this body had been bleeding out for hours at this point; any mana used needed strategical implementation, not scratching at inches thick ropes embedded into flesh. The trick was to get her into my form, was part of the reason I'd established it to begin with. "You lied. You said you'd prevent this." There was a hiss in Kisate's voice. "Who are you *really*? What do you really want?"

*"That's not what I said."* I had been rather particular about what I promised: I never said that Kylie wouldn't be kidnapped, that Asuza wouldn't find her. If anything, I was rather certain I had implied the opposite, that Asuza was actively searching, that we needed to be ready.

I said that Kylie wouldn't die. And for the record, she did still draw breath, so there were no broken promises. I just needed the last piece to fall into place now: I needed Rota and Jordan here for a mana transfer before Kylie's body shut down.

# Chapter Thirty-Eight

## blinking lights

Jordan | June 26
Training House

Kylie was over half an hour late, something that'd never happened in all the years I'd known her — not at school, not the hangouts we'd had over the years, and certainly not these imposed training sessions. Even if she wanted to skip, my impression's Siani would've given her hell over it. She'd had a lot on her mind, though, and maybe the *others* couldn't wake each other up. I didn't know since the freeloaders in my head had never woken me up.

Speaking of quiet, Rotanu still hadn't said much, and it'd been a damn blessing.

Not sure what else to do, I left the training house, encountering no protests when I did so. Prob'ly 'cause she was late and the apartment'd been a fuckin' zoo with everyone trying to pack shit. I was surprised I'd even managed to sneak out as it was, and I certainly ain't rushing back to that hellhole today. As I wandered past the park, my feet took me to her house on instinct. I wasn't exactly a welcome guest if Ms. Rae answered, but something just felt *off* 'bout Kylie being this late.

The streets were quiet, not much conversation between the

voices that normally never shut up. Something was strange, intimidating almost.

Blinking lights, red and blue. I saw 'em flash from a distance. My heart raced. Picking up my pace, I saw lights where I least wanted 'em: two police cars parked in the driveway of Kylie's town home.

My throat went dry. My legs wouldn't move, not closer or further or anything. Why're they here?

Where was she? Why was she late?

I searched the driveway for answers, noticing a presence by the front door: Dani. She briefly made eye contact with me b'fore running out with red eyes and cheeks. "Where is she?" She demanded an answer, as if I had one, as if I wasn't there asking the same question.

I shook my head. How'd I know?

It's all a mistake.

She grabbed my shoulders, fingers tightly gripping my shirt fabric. "Why won't you say anything?! All she ever said was how it wasn't a problem, that *you'd* or Rota or whoever the fuck would save her if it came to that and *where is she?!*"

Dani could yell and yell. I had no answer. How could I?

*"She... she can't be... We'd know, we'd have notice this time..."* Takite said.

Rotanu didn't give a sarcastic quip. Didn't reassure anyone. He said nothing.

Dani lowered her head, a much weaker, softer, vulnerable in her voice as she choked, "Please... She trusted you."

Kylie wouldn't have — couldn't have — trusted me for any of this. But something's wrong, something I'd noticed since yesterday: Rotanu'd been quiet, distant, distracted.

I didn't know anything.

But *Rotanu* did.

Not believing I was even asking this, I did so anyways: "You knew, didn't you, Rotanu? You fuckin' *knew.* Why didn't you say anything? Why didn't you...?"

*"...'Cause I trust Kyle."*

*"You aren't serious, Rota?! Don't you understand what's happened?! We were trusting your memory to... to..."* John yelled.

Rotanu knew when we left the previous day that Kylie'd be

kidnapped. Rotanu knew when I was packing shit and sleeping and, fuck, even walking to that damn house.

Rotanu knew. And he didn't say a damn fuckin' thing.

"This's how the others died, ain't it?" My voice was soft, but I wasn't trying to hide the info from Dani; I couldn't be bothered hiding anything right then. It was the slow realization, the fear I saw in her eyes as she cried freshly playing through my mind. Rotanu *let* this happen. "Is... is she...?" The word was harsh on my ears: "Dead?"

Dani's eyes widened, arms dropping. "No, you can't — she can't, it's your fault if... if..."

*"She can't be,"* Rotanu said. *"The connection keeping me here's dependent on her being alive. Connection's still stable, but if we're doing this, you need to get your ass in gear. Now."*

# Chapter Thirty-Nine
## dark red wires

Kylie | June 26
Asuza's Castle

Everything ached; I felt exhausted, even more fatigued than the Initial Cycle, which previously held the record for the worst lethargy of my life. Opening my eyes, I saw an ever so slight smear across my vision, like a paintbrush that pulled colors slightly outside the lines. Trying to reposition my posture, I couldn't; my mind woke to further pain, to this stab — no, multiple stabs — in my back, shirt risen to my lower ribs to accommodate whatever was stuck in me. Some kind of rope pinned my torso against this chair, preventing any adjustment at all, digging into my ribs. Now-warm metal had long since formed marks on my forearms and lower calves. My head was the only thing I could move, seeing these dark red wires surround me. I rapidly glanced away to bite back the urge to throw up, realizing the wires themselves weren't actually red — they were clear. The red was because of what was inside them.

And not in me any longer: my blood.

*"Amazing he's had two-thousand years, and this is 'humane, fast' option he's come up with. Definitely wasn't at the top of his class,"* Sia said.

If Sia was awake, why was I tied up?

mentioned over and over again. The man who had murdered Leah, had murdered Chloé. Was in the process of murdering me.

He shook his head, frigid nose brushing against my hand from his proximity to my face. He had no breath, no rise and fall of his chest. "Ku taiwuasii, sikira sote. Wa ku tainorerukuzo taikesekuzo udeumuidayu sawaranikuzo neadaro wara edatara."

Kisate rapidly lost control of my body, Sia weaving herself in effortlessly. "Taiwearoi taateiruroi soaroesatu taotai takaekai rae." Wait, all this time, *Sia* knew Riyatian too? Even with her comments to Kisate that it wasn't important... Sia was at least fluent enough to have no trouble with the sounds or finding words to say.

Yet another kiss to my hand, this one right beside my absorption device, still on my finger from when I placed it there earlier after the chain had snapped. "Re koatease, sikira keekayi."

Sia moved her eyes to the green-eyed woman hidden by shadows. "Iwuki somiria anawi aroesatuyu." Her head gestured to the woman, a slight tilt up.

"Nimaka?" he asked.

"Nu uridi sikieyu kuwoureki, kaa..." There was a meekness, almost a vulnerability, to Sia's tone. What was she even saying? What had Sia this submissive? "Kaa..." Sia sniffled. Was Sia crying? What had happened?

Out of the corner of Sia's vision, I saw the man glance up at Sia's face and then turn to face the woman. "Sikira keekayi? Taiweakuzo soari arasuyu?"

"Notaonakoroi sikie someteowayo, mu ateitu notamiweroi zeeki hekowoyu neadaro sikie mu notakaekuroi eru notaedatai notanukei soeseyu nuna wiekier rae."

He stood, swiftly walking to the woman; Sia relinquished control, Kisate gaining it since she last had control.

"Master Asuza?" the woman asked.

His palm slammed against her cheek, throwing her to the cobbled stone flooring. "You ungrateful wench. How *dare* you even think to address Her Highness as such, and to purposefully injure her... You were graced even to touch her skin, yet you..." He pulled her up by her hair. "We'll speak on this later, get out of this room: you are never to approach Her Highness again."

*"Oh yeah. That was one-hundred percent worth it."* The previous timidness from Sia vanished and was replaced by a smug tone.

What had she said? What had just happened?

Either way, both *visitors* left. Kisate had control of my body, but the room was silent, only the sound of rolling waves further indicating I was nowhere near home.

# Chapter Forty

## advantages

There were only two people I knew better than myself, and one of them owed me like hell right then 'cause I felt damn ice projectiles in my general direction. When *Jordan* was the one most receptive, it said something.

This's standard mode operandi for her but didn't mean I *liked* it. Unfortunately, I knew and understood *why* it had to be like this: one of the primary reasons — and the one that ultimately pushed me into agreeing to this shit show — was that we didn't know *exactly* when this jackass was gonna be here outside of this time under this circumstance.

Besides, if I was going against her, it ain't on this plan; others're more necessary, so I trusted in my memory, in *her*.

In myself.

With all the chaos around Kylie's town home, no one besides Dani noticed when I took over Jordan's body to transform into Jordan's "alt form" — the simulation of my body and mana supply. The mana from the latter enabled me to teleport, something Jordan wouldn't learn for years to come. I arrived here, at this old castle — castle might've been a stretch actually: pure stone walls like most around it, but judging by

# Chapter Forty-One
## reverse link

Jordan | June 26
Asuzás Castle

I wasn't sure why *I* got assigned a task yet Dmitri got nothing. Wasn't I the most inexperienced? Regardless, Rotanu didn't ask permission or even pretend to wait for an answer as he shoved me back in charge of my body.

On top of that... I didn't get what Rotanu meant by not trusting my senses, or if I should trust anything he said to begin with: He'd allowed all this to happen... to risk Kylie's life. Yet...

What other choice did I have? I didn't know where the fuck I even was — withered grass, ocean for what looked like miles. Opal Pines's at least an hour away from the closest coastline; I wasn't sure how he'd done it, but I was nowhere near the city I'd grown up in, and it'd happened in a matter of *seconds*. Wasn't much longer than the time he'd even been in his form, actually: that transformation still winded the fuck outta me whenever he released it, so it would've been nice if he didn't fuckin' switch for thirty seconds then change his damn mind. Whatever, though: I liked being *myself*, not him. Had only briefly experienced controlling that body, and it's strange as fuck, and —

A brief silence reminded me of the moment's seriousness. It

wasn't time for bitching. I swallowed, opening the large wooden door. Torches lined both sides of the hallway, only 'bout half of 'em actually lit. There're stone walls and flooring. Even if just for a second, the beauty of the building struck me, of architecture like I'd never seen. Of the heaviest door I'd ever touched.

Taking a cautious step in, I didn't notice anything wrong with my senses — could see normally considering that this hallway was dimly lit, so obscured vision made sense. Was this another lie from Rotanu? I could hear waves still rolling against the shoreline from outside. Could smell both the salt from the ocean — something I'd experienced only once or twice prior when I was much younger and went on a mandatory field trip for class — and musk and... decay?

Where's decay coming from?

Another few steps in, a large stone altar. A girl's on top, reddish brown shoulder-length hair, hands placed on her chest.

Kylie...?

*"That... that bastard..."* Dmitri said. It was the first time I'd heard him cuss.

I stepped closer — was it Kylie? For second it was, but just as quickly, became the original girl once more. A third girl — no, this one's a woman, reddish brown hair down to her arms — flashed in my sight.

Why're none of the others saying anything?

Another step forward.

Another flash in my vision: this time of a chair and the first girl with shoulder-length hair tied up, crying. Her head slumped forward; no more tears came. A sharp pain in my chest left me gasping. My vision blurred as the girl switched to the woman with longer hair who now had scrape marks against her left cheek, tied to a chair in a similar position as the girl that'd been crying. That sharp pain — a stab, not a hit, not like I was more familiar with — pierced deeper into my chest, like it went through my heart and through my back, more black spots invading my vision, leading me to close my eyes between the pain and disorientation from black spots encroaching in.

*"Break..."* A female voice? It almost sounded like —

Kylie?

I opened my eyes back, pain vanished and vision fine, a slight gasp through my mouth.

"Nice nap there," Kylie teased.

What?

Focusing my eyes, I saw my tenth-grade math room, a place I hadn't been to in almost a month. "You're okay?" I asked. I didn't know how or why we're there, but Rotanu had taken me away instantly, so me being back in a classroom just as quickly wasn't impossible. Should've been impossible, but that was fuckin' everything these past few months. The others're still silent, so must've been preoccupied as hell to not be as relieved as me right then. Or maybe that's why they're silent.

Her head tilted to the side. "Why wouldn't I be?"

"I mean, you'd gone missing, and... fuck, it just... scared the shit outta me." I didn't mean for my eyes to water.

'Til recently, she'd been the only person to talk to me like an actual person. Who thought I could be someone. Was worth something.

She's the person I valued most, and that's why Rotanu couldn't be my future. I wasn't worthy of someone like her, no matter how much I —

"How hard were you dreaming?" She laughed, shifting the weight of her backpack.

Backpack? School'd been out for over a month, and we had another month b'fore it started back. I lowered my eyes, trying to process the information in front of me and what it meant. "Dumb question, but what's today's date?"

"March 24th, why?"

The day I went with her to the park, wanting to hang out even a few minutes longer b'fore going home for the weekend; I knew she'd just be waiting for Dani, but I'm never in a rush to go home. It was something that'd had happened hundreds of times prior to that day — to the attack where that little red-haired shit and her hellspawn oversized housecat almost killed us.

It's like none of it'd happened.

"I just..." I didn't know the fuck's going on. Had the entire past four months been a vivid dream? I wasn't that creative. Lied like shit. There's no way I could've made it up.

"Wow, I want that kind of nap. This is why you're struggling in class, you know."

She wasn't really wrong there. "Yeah, yeah." Wasn't like anyone expected me to make it outta high school anyways.

"Anyway, I'm heading out; he's waiting for me. Just didn't want to leave you passed out there." She waved before walking off.

She was a few steps away before I asked, "'He'?" Was it a lab partner in one of her honors classes again? And actually, why're we meeting in *math*? That's my sixth period class; English's my eighth — final — period class, and she's implying we're done for the day.

Rolling her eyes, she huffed. "You really *were* out. It's been a few weeks already since he and I started going out, remember? We were about to start our walk home together, but I saw you there and didn't want to just leave you for who knows how long. Good thing too, with how out of it you are."

What?

In all the years I'd known her, she'd never gone out with anyone. Hadn't ever even expressed an interest in anyone. We'd grown up together, me seeing guys ask her out over the years, and everyone of them turned down.

That's why Rotanu and Siani couldn't't've been together. Not just dating but *engaged*. Bullshit. I knew it's bullshit. And yet...

The warmth in Siani's eyes, her quiet plead to let her help me.

It'd been hope. A moment that I'm *worth a damn* to someone. A promise that I'd one day be the most important person to the person most important to me.

All I could do's say, "What?"

She didn't hear me, waving as she said, "See you," and walked out of the room.

My eyes further watered, felt like my heart had stopped if not shattered. It's enough. It's enough to just be by her side. I shouldn't — *couldn't* — ask for more.

*"Jordan..."*

She'd already left; why was I hearing her call my name? Some fuckin' cruel joke of my brain, prob'ly. I sniffled, eyes closing as I rubbed them.

My head banged into something hard.

Yelping from the unexpected pain, I smelt alcohol before my

eyes opened. I identified the object I'd collided into's the oven door , pulsing pain shooting throughout my head and into my limbs.

"You damn useless piece of shit." My father's fist slammed into my jaw. How none of my teeth broke from the impact, I wasn't sure. "You thought you'd get outta here?" My father threw me into the cold gray tile of our apartment kitchen. The cheap, sterile white overhead light shone down. "You thought she'd actually *like* someone like you?"

No, of course not. Of course she wouldn't. Not like that. I was fortunate she even liked me as a friend, tolerated my existence.

"Of course I don't. It's just pity." Glancing up, I saw her there, jean shorts and tank top on, sitting on the kitchen counter by the fridge. I shakily stood, watching her swing her legs back and forth.

Why's she here? She'd never known where I lived — how *could* she when I could barely keep up with moving somewhere else as soon as I'd learned the address? "Kylie...?"

Another huff and roll of her eyes as she jumped down from the counter and walked beside my father. "You were so pathetic, I had to entertain you. But *you* thought someone like *me* would want to date you? That's *hilarious*. You aren't even worthy of being my friend, let alone anything else."

It wasn't wrong.

Why *had* I thought anything else? It'd all been a lie. A false hope. *"Seriously, Jordan!"*

That wasn't Kylie's voice. It was older, more mature. Cynical yet soft.

Warmth burned against my chest, just above my heart — it didn't hurt, was a comforting burn somehow. But what would've caused that sensation? Reaching just below my neck, I felt the necklace Kylie had given me for my sixteenth birthday; the pendant's far warmer than it should've been from naturally being pressed against my skin. It wasn't painful, though, was just short of hot, like being in front of a heater after a long stint outside in the cold.

Like mana coursing through me.

Was it all a lie?

Was the past four months a nightmare or what I felt right then the nightmare?

Wasn't this better, her safe? Wasn't this how it's always meant to be?

Her eyes were cruel, distant, sneering as she stared at me.

She'd never looked at me that way. Never in the eight years I'd known her — she's too kind to look at anyone like that.

If the past four months're a lie, then I had no magic. Then Siani and Rotanu'd never existed.

But it wasn't a lie, was it?

Holding my right hand out, palm up, I willed for a flame as Takite'd taught me. I panted as a flame emerged above my hand. No pain, just warmth.

That's my truth.

This's what Rotanu had meant, that voice calling for me's Siani — she needed us. Me. And I wouldn't let the reality in front of me become real.

Closing my eyes, I focused on that flame and expanded it over and over and over, fire encasing me as shallow breaths heaved from my chest and sweat dripped down my forehead.

A dark stone room, a stone altar with a girl on top, shoulder-length reddish brown hair.

I fell to my knees, gasping as I did my best to force air into my lungs.

*"How the fuck did she...?"* Rotanu said, almost under his breath. *"She held...? Fuckin' hell that's smooth, to reverse link the connection for subcon access to utilize instinctual... Damn."*

I didn't know what Rotanu's saying and quite frankly, didn't give a damn. I'd never admit it, but I was just glad to hear him at all: this's my reality, and Kylie's still alive if Rotanu's present. There's still time.

# Chapter Forty-Two

## those that still have blood

There's no way Asuza hadn't noticed Jordan's aura spiking, so the final timer had started; as it was, I'd barely been able to disrupt that trap spell for the brief seconds I had, and even that had taken multiple attempts and used up the emergency mana rations Kylie had that I wasn't supposed to know about. The strategy had been successful: I used the connection from Riyati that sustained Rota to break into Jordan's subcon, but there were definitely drawbacks to that method given it'd completely drained Kyle's reserves. I *couldn't wait* for Kisate to figure out I did that one.

Regardless, I was still proud of Jordan, could feel determination despite the fatigue from disrupting the trap field. It'd captured the whole Kaku Tiza line, but only Jordan could physically break it, being the one in control. I admired the art of Asuza's trap but was less than amused dealing with disrupting it and knowing the emotional strain on its victims.

On Jordan and Rota, and I'd be lying if I said I had no idea of what Rota had seen, of my role in them. I wished there was time to comfort them, reach out to hold and soothe them.

But I couldn't.

Kylie had probably an hour of consciousness left, if that, and only a few hours before her body shut down. Things were down to the wire. I'd now done all I could do for now: Rota and Jordan needed to get a mana transfer up to the connection point, and the faster they got here, the better our odds given Asuza wasn't that far away either.

The wooden door creaked open; Kylie controlled her body because Kisate, Leah, and Chloé were near to rather irritating hysterics; I was unfortunately rather preoccupied with mana presentation and dedicating extra focus toward the Riyati link that sustained Rota and myself.

At least the other three kept Kylie conscious with their carrying on.

Kylie opened her eyes, but as expected, her vision was out of focus. I used auras to confirm the one who opened the door was Jordan, but it also confirmed that at the rate of Asuza's aura movement, he was only three minutes away at best.

This was going to be fun.

*"Just a bit more, Kylie,"* I said.

*"What, 'til she joins us?"* Leah snapped. Her support through this was endearing, very helpful.

Cautious footsteps edged closer and closer, a dim dark red and blue aura: Jordan. Rota's form would've been extra strain on Kylie, so Rota knew, unfortunately, this mana transfer had to come out of Jordan's supply.

Those footsteps edged even closer, each one timid and afraid, until he was right where Kylie was tied down. "You're fuckin' with me," he stammered.

Now was *not* the time for their spats, and if I could've reached out to yell at them, I would've. I couldn't, though; I had to wait, to trust. And I still hated waiting as much as I hated mornings and getting out of bed.

*"They're too late. She's... there's no way..."* Chloé cried while speaking, which made her difficult to understand and wasn't exactly helpful in keeping Kylie calm; fear expended more mana, and extra mana usage was the top of the "don't do this" list right then.

"Dammit," Jordan whispered as he stepped even closer, his breath on her cheek. His lips touched her hot skin; Kylie wasn't lucid enough to notice him there. That didn't matter: the mana transfer had begun. This was checkmate; Rota would hold the mana transfer as long as he could on his end so as not to alert Asuza any faster, thus delaying Jordan and Kylie's auras spiking.

A minute passed. Sweat dripped from Jordan's hairline onto Kylie's knee. Jordan already had less time to acclimate to magic compared to Kylie, and that was ignoring his max magipoten was lower than Kylie's own; most of his mana would get transferred to get her out of critical status. His head lowered, gasps from his lungs. His legs dropped as his head slammed into Kylie's thighs. I wasn't sure if Rota intended for Jordan to break contact right there, but we had to go with it; I prepared for the aura spike that would come once Rota stopped interrupting the mana transfer process. As expected, Jordan's aura spiked before resonating with Kylie's; mana flowed into her, and Kylie's consciousness began steadying.

Now it was our turn. My turn.

Heavy footsteps echoed into the room: Asuza; Jordan must not have closed the door behind him. "You won't make her!" he screamed, rushing toward the barely conscious Jordan.

Splitting control with Kylie, I focused my eyes on Jordan; he was vulnerable, still wheezing from the amount of mana he had transferred and lost.

Asuza swung a pike at Jordan's neck. There were few lines never meant to be crossed, and hurting Jordan was the first: I generated a barrier around Jordan. When Asuza connected with the barrier, the force threw him back against the stone wall, a snap that probably was his spine. Didn't matter since he was dead and all, but still wasn't the most pleasant sound.

*"You just used?! She's about dead and you... you..."* Chloé hadn't realized, wasn't trained enough to notice that Kylie didn't have enough mana to generate that strength of barrier even if she had been full on mana. Asuza would've easily pierced any barrier Kylie created.

*"How...?"* Kisate's first non-hysteric words in hours. I felt the realization ebbing from her; it was a distinct emotion to pick up compared to the exhaustion and panic from everyone else around. *"She shouldn't... even if he got some through..."*

*"Told you all to shut up because I had it under control."* I

**215**

*"Kisate, one thing you should know."* I didn't know why I bothered telling her this. Why now and not before? Why at all? Honestly, I wasn't sure. I just knew it felt right. *"Notaikuroi mietumu sokiseti aroesato neadaro soamoyu. Ku tumeroidi kaa rae, ku koarosa."*

A choked sob escaped from Kisate as she repeated, *"Thank you. For everything."*

And then they were gone, no longer consciousnesses among the living. The glyph closed, Jordan and Kylie falling against each other.

As they would both live another day.

# Chapter Forty-Three

## just one hour

*"Once she releases Kyle's form, she's gonna need a hell'va heal. I'm gonna take over to heal her,"* I said to Jordan; I seriously doubted he'd fight me given he was exhausted and wanted to collapse. For once, I didn't blame him.

"Mm." Jordan had his right hand over his temple as an attempt to stop the throbbing headache from high mana consumption on top of having three souls ripped out of his body; I wasn't thrilled at the physiological kickback I'd just signed up for, but it was what it was.

After assuming control, I tightened my eyes: as expected, muscles were strained and everything hurt like fuck. One problem at a time, with the first being these damn wings. I took a deep breath and dismissed them, gaining the benefit of no longer fighting for space with Kyle's wings and reabsorbing the mana that comprised their physical presence.

Opening and then focusing my eyes, I watched the woman in front of me: slow, even breaths, left fist tightening before supporting herself to a standing position. Kyle. Kylie wouldn't've had that damn near inhuman control. Further confirmation: her wings dismissed, something only Kyle'd know how to do.

She offered her hand to me, and I took it as she helped me stand to my feet. "This's why we don't let you call any damn shots."

She chuckled as she rolled her eyes. "It worked, didn't it?"

"And we both look and fuckin' feel like shit."

That damn coy glint in her eyes as she shrugged. "Sounds like Tuesday to me." Also that's the goddamn problem: she wasn't *wrong* there, and it's why I hated when she made plans.

Jordan didn't even have the mental capacity to remark on my exchange with her. He hadn't collapsed yet, but his mental capacity's shot to hell from everything that'd happened. I was prob'bly gonna get stuck on damn packing duty 'cause shit still needed packing b'fore moving happened again.

But... that could wait. Despite the obvious fatigue, Kyle was at peace; this meant more to her than me. My closure came from memories instead of goodbyes. "Not staying, I assume," I said.

She nodded with a hesitance I'm sure she'd deny. "It's not time yet. For now... let's go home." She offered her hand to me so we'd split the teleport cost; I should've known she'd realized my mana supply's shot since her empathy had to be active as fuck right then.

Taking her hand, she shifted the mana requirements off me as our surrounding's shifted to Opal Pines. Specifically, the training house, empty as always. As soon as the teleport finished, she swayed.

Dammit, she'd taken too much of the overhead again. Holding her arms, I steadied her, slowly releasing as she regained her balance. "Kyle..."

"It's fine." It's never fine when she said that. Usually it meant I had a hell'va headache on my hands. "I'm about to release anyways; there's no real cleanup in this form, just hers."

Sighing, I nodded: this ain't an argument I'd win, and I'm well aware of it. Her form shifted to Kylie's.

*"Fuck..."* Jordan said as my eyes ran over Kylie's body: it was far from the worst I'd seen, but there're scars Kyle still had on her body from this fiasco in our time, especially around her wrists and ankles, where right then blood dripped across broken skin.

Kyle crouched on the concrete, blood dripping every damn where. The slightest wince escaped her lips as she flexed her fingers slowly, likely trying to regain movement after they'd been tied down so long.

I kneeled beside her as I laid my right hand over her left ankle. She shook her head. "Not yet."

"What?"

"Most of this needs to stay. She was kidnapped and ran away from said captors. Biggest cleanup is her back, not hiding that she was tied up."

Just because she's right didn't mean I *liked it*. "Fine, lemme get your, her, fuck English, gimme your back. You look like shit, and if you look like shit, she's not..." I didn't know how to finish that sentence, not with Jordan and Kylie around: Kyle's pain thresholds're insanely high. Much higher than anything Kylie could tolerate. Me and Kyle knew that if she's feeling pain, Kylie'd likely black out if she got control back. That felt wrong to admit in front of them, though.

Kyle sighed before she nodded. I moved behind her, lifting her shirt up with my left hand.

*"Wait, wait."* Jordan shouted as if the sight of Kylie's back's something explicit, the entrance to a sight we're barred. *"The fuck're you...? I don't care if it's Siani in control, don't you —"*

That might be the most argumentative I'd seen him, and it's a hell've a show. "You want her to keep bleeding out?"

*"Of course not, it's just..."*

Kyle held the shirt to where I'd lifted it, freeing my left hand. "She's out, so no complaints here, too bad."

"Oh, shuddup." She ain't having fun outta the hell I'm getting from him over this, 'specially not as I unhooked her bra, fully exposing her bare back. Dried blood, little injection marks across her skin, centered around the left and right of her spine.

*"The fuck're you both...?"*

"It's okay, Jordan," Kyle said with a chuckle. "Kylie's very low on mana, even with the transfer from you. Rota's just healing where they were blood-draining her."

Like a switch, Jordan changed from embarrassed, protective, and getting hot over just a damn bare back to silent. How's she so damn good she stopped an argument she couldn't even hear?

didn't know the privilege of hearing that tone, of how I'd worked my ass off for her to trust me enough for moments like these.

I tightened my grip, my fingers between hers. "Give us an hour. Just one." I didn't know who I was asking permission from: Jordan, Kylie, Kyle, or even myself.

*"An hour? For what?"*

She nodded, laying her forehead on my shoulder. "You win."

Jordan could figure it out. Hell, he could go to sleep or process things or whatever the fuck he wanted as long as he shut up and didn't ruin this. Emotions counted too 'cause she sure as fuck's reading us right then.

I released my hand from hers, bringing her into a close hug. This wasn't us: we were shorter and younger. But it's enough, for just a moment.

*"Ah, oh..."* Jordan's uncomfortable, and if I was in a more charitable mood, I would've understood why: Jordan's the awkward third wheel, and he didn't have much choice given he felt the hug and scent of blood and soft hair, just a muted version of it all. *Jordan* wasn't close enough to Kylie for this, but Kylie ain't conscious and Jordan could shut the hell up for a damn minute.

Another chuckle from Kyle. "Sorry, Jordan. I just... consider it a favor, please."

I struggled against the instinct to move my lips to hers. It wasn't time. Wasn't right. I compromised by kissing her forehead. She pecked my cheek softly. Then we stood, just like that, our arms around each other. No words needed.

I knew it wasn't the last time. She knew it's only the beginning. But we'd survived something no incarnation b'fore us had. It was okay to take a moment and acknowledge that. To let Kylie rest b'fore going back into her life, seeing the chaos caused by events her mother'd never truly know or understand. To give Jordan hope, even if he's a dumbass who'd deny it for years 'cause he's an idiot.

To give myself just a moment of being me, who once again nearly lost the woman I loved, who'd seen visions of her death over and over, of how cold Chloé's lips'd been when Dmitri tried to rush to her, to kiss her as if it'd wake her from a spell. But there's no spell; she's no faerie tale princess, and I'd never been a prince charming. Chloé didn't wake up; Dmitri followed like John, saw the sword left on the stone ground, likely intentionally placed there after Asuza watched John's reaction to Leah's death. Struck true until my gasps stopped and my own lips grew cold.

I'd stayed quiet 'cause I trusted her, trusted in her resilience and strength and her faith in Jordan, in myself. But fuckin' hell'd I been terrified and just wanted to stay with her that day to prevent Kylie ever experiencing what she'd just felt, what Kyle and me knew happened from here. Asuza's gone, good riddance to a man that murdered without remorse. The incarnations that'd been trapped by him and even the ones prior able to rest, no longer spectators trapped in a body.

Yet...

It wasn't easier from here, and I didn't know the right path forward.

227

This back and forth of details that were vague and at best half-truths continued, Sia crying and hesitating and stumbling as if it was genuine, as if Sia wasn't the only one that had maintained composure during the entire event. Maybe Rota too, but his emotions had at least flickered, doubt and fear intermixed; Sia — the brief glances I had felt — had no such hesitation. And I wished I was upset about that; maybe once I had rested, I would be. As it was, I wished I could've processed and felt even half the emotion that Sia displayed. My emotions were utterly tapped out, exhaustion in all forms of the word.

All I wanted was to be held by Mom while crawling into my bed. Not to be here, pretending like the police would ever catch a now permanently deceased attacker, one that the person speaking to them had assured would never be a problem again. Not in trying to acknowledge some of these lies I probably should've paid attention to because I'd be asked about them later and honestly had no recollection of whatever Sia was saying. Maybe that could be part of my *symptoms* that would no doubt be put in a file and get Mom's attention for the next —

...Mom was going to be miserable once we went home. I didn't want to leave my house for a week, but I could already tell I'd be lucky if I was allowed out by the time school started back.

"I just..." Sia's voice was soft, this hint of vulnerability. A complete lie. "Can I go home now?" She lowered her hands into her lap, sniffling. "Please. I don't... I just want to go home."

Resignation. They actually fell for that.

"All right. If you remember anything else, call me," Mrs. Alana said.

Sia nodded, rubbing her nose with her wrist. She stood, a hesitation and shake to each step. As she stumbled to the door and opened it, Dani rushed, tightly hugging her.

Of course, *that* was when Sia pushed me back in control, as if I had the fortitude to deal with anyone right then.

*"I did my part. It's not like I'm wide awake here either."*

I didn't buy it, didn't buy Sia couldn't have held out ten more minutes or however long until we got home. I also didn't have the capacity to even attempt to argue, instead standing at the door and then a bit to the side so the adults could leave.

For the first time in our lives, I heard a tremble in Dani's voice as she said, "I was so scared."

It hadn't clicked that the last time we'd talked was when I had walked out. From Dani's perspective, I could've died without us ever making up. I got it. I just couldn't process it, feel relief right then. The connection between logic and my emotions had never felt so disjointed. "Y-yeah," I said, returning the hug before pulling away and hoping for Dani to get the hint.

Mrs. Alana whispered to Mom, "Something isn't right. Keep your eyes on her."

"You think she...?"

"I don't think she ran away, she's not that type of girl, and she couldn't have caused those wounds to herself. There's some outside force involved. I'm hoping her memory stabilizes, because right now we have no leads. Poor thing's exhausted though, so I don't think pushing her further is going to help anything."

Finally, I could just go home.

me. "Sia knew too. Was calm through the whole thing. And I want to be angry, be betrayed, and I don't understand *why* it needed to be like that, why no one gave heads up or *anything*, but..." Another nod. Was it to me? To herself? Fuck if I knew at this point. "Kisate... Leah and Chloé... I think Takite, John, and Dmitri too... They didn't want to be here anymore. It was for them. I think."

Rotanu said nothing, offered no insight into Kylie's deductions and their accuracy. I wished he would've, if only to bridge the otherwise lapse in conversation that was hidden by the tv.

"Are *you* gonna be all right though?" I didn't know what else to say, to ask, to change the topic.

She shrugged. "I'm exhausted. Had nightmares last night, and I know I slept through most of that, um, day, compared to Sia — she went to bed *before* me last night, which like never happens. I think so though, or I will be. I think... wait..." Her eyes widened — had Sia said something? It'd have been nice if Rotanu and Siani could extend their *voices* at least to Kylie and me together. Instead, we could only get half the conversation at once. Her lips pressed together. "What about you? Like, you went through a lot of mana yourself, and... and did you have to go to the station too? You weren't gone long enough to be noticed, right?"

Rotanu chuckled. *"Damn, she's adorable."* I hated I agreed, if for nothing else than the fact that she'd never caught on to anything with my home life being so drastically different than her own. Maybe it's 'cause we met so young, she'd just never thought otherwise. Whatever the case, I preferred it this way, her the one part of my life where I just *was*.

"Ah, uh. Nah. Wasn't gone long enough, yeah." It'd prob'ly take weeks b'fore anyone in my house'd notice, let alone if they'd bother filing anything; most likely wouldn't bother, and I knew it. It's the difference between our lives, something only Kylie's unaware of outta the people in the room; Siani knew and stayed true to her word of not saying anything to Kylie. And Rotanu, well. Most useful thing to come outta any of this's at least Rotanu knew healing magic to help after I got the shit beat outta me; not going around in pain for weeks's the only good thing in this, actually.

Sighing, she rolled her eyes. "Fine, go ahead. Not like you've bothered to teach me how anyways."

Her eyes hardened, the hesitance in her wrists relaxing.

*"Kyle? What'd they switch for?"*

Hell if I knew; I wasn't even positive it's Siani, though Rotanu's usually pretty accurate in deciphering between the two. "It's going to be a second before she can train with you again."

Of fuckin' course it's 'bout work. I should've guessed; that's an entirely too Kylie-like behavior I wished had changed, but Siani indicated it only got worse. "Y-yeah, she needs rest after..."

Siani shook her head.

*"You think Kyle believes in 'rest' and taking it easy? You're hilarious."*

Rotanu was, yet again, *not helping.*

"More like... independent study for a bit. Not for her physical recovery but well." Her eyes went toward the direction of the kitchen.

*"Ah. Yeah, not wrong. Her mom's prob'ly had a bitch-fit in a half from this as it is... no way in hell she's sneaking around the city for a bit."*

"Rest's good," I said. It'd give me time to move yet again, too. Couldn't've been many damn places left in this city.

A slight smirk pulled at Siani's lips. "That does mean you both need to actually, you know, *study*. And I'm not talking about *her* and you."

I wanted to say "fuck you" to Siani at the implication I needed to work with Rotanu. Unfortunately, I was neither that direct or brave and instead just lowered my gaze from her.

*"Nailed us there..."* Rotanu said.

"But that's not today." Siani said. "And Rota... three weeks I think, if you wouldn't mind."

*"Damn, she calling it early."*

"What d'you...?"

An aggravated huff. "She won't answer. Said she needs some rest, which isn't even a *good* lie."

I wasn't ready to accept that this was my new normal. That Siani and Rotanu were my future. But even if just for a moment — a moment I'd never admit to Rotanu... Maybe it wouldn't be such a bad future if it was, if this warmth was something I freely received like never b'fore.

If I'm allowed by her side for even a few more years.

# *thanks for reading!*

Thank you for reading until the end! If you enjoyed this story, please consider leaving a review on Goodreads, TheStoryGraph, BookBub, PageBound, or on your favorite book retailer — as you've likely heard many times, reviews are exceptionally important for indie authors, and each one both means a ton and is super helpful in helping others decide if this book is right for them!

Check riyati.ink/rebirth for a handy list of review sites & retailers!

# *acknowledgements*

One of the biggest lessons I learned while writing *Riyati Rebirth* is that no book is written alone, regardless of what it says on the cover. I'd like to take this opportunity to thank many of the individuals that helped bring this book to life. Foremost, I want to thank all three of my cats, who graciously allowed me time from praising their existence long enough to get words on a page, and even more specifically, my black cat Krishna, who encouraged me throughout the entire process by sleeping on my feet dutifully, no matter how hot it was (he's a very dedicated little void). Next, I would like to thank my husband and closest friends: thank you to my husband, who has watched me stumble, fall, and struggle to get back up over and over, for continuously believing in me and encouraging me for almost a decade and a half now. To my two closest friends, I — let alone this book — might not be here today if it wasn't for you always supporting me and standing by me.

Next, I'd like to make special mention to Ka'ua Lara and Alli Rense for graciously beta reading this book to refine it into what's here today, and to Alli for the guidance she provided not only with the beta but my personal website and Riyati's series website — it only looks as good as it does because of you! This book may well have not been possible with the continued support and listening ears from the Evil Writer's Society discord, who have endured countless hours of my ranting, squealing, and probably more screenshots than they ever cared to see because I do love posting those. I'd like to shout out Creepyllama, who brought my characters to life with her beautiful renders that are in Campfire Edition of *Riyati Rebirth* and are part of Riyati's Library Archive. I'd also like to thank Emory Glass for the phenomenal first edition cover, and amagren for the glyph illustrations used in the second edition's cover. As well, I'd like to thank Dax Murray, whose wisdom with self-publishing helped me avoid at least 400% of the errors I was about to make as a complete newbie to this publishing thing. Last but not least for specific individuals, I'd like to thank my undergraduate creative nonfiction professor: thank you for seeing potential when none of the other professors did and encouraging me in finding my own path with writing.

I'd be remiss to not thank the stories of my youth and stories that still guide me today, that provided a dawn even when things were bleak. Finally, I appreciate every reader that picks up this book, I'd love to hear what you thought about *Riyati Rebirth* — I only bite sometimes, I promise!

Sincerely,
Kai Zeal

# *about the author*

Kai Zeal (she/her) is a queer, disabled writer, academic, gamer, cat mom, and, most recently, content creator. She got her start writing fanfiction as a child, creating an awareness of tropes, characterization, and the importance of retellings. From there, she refined her analytical skills both in academia and through fandom with critical analysis of media to gain a better understanding of how the parts of a work come together to form its whole.

She has degrees in psychology, writing, higher education administration, and is pursuing a PhD with a research focus on critical disability studies through a queer, feminist lens. In her free time, she's a lifelong gamer, particularly of JRPGs, many of which have shaped her storytelling strategies and love of media.

Want to know more? Check out her personal website & sign up for her monthly newsletter at https://kai-zeal.com/. For *Riyati* specific information, check out https://riyati.ink/

# interested in more riyati?

If you'd like to further explore Opal Pines and the *Riyati* universe, sign up for my newsletter to receive *Riyati Origins*! You'll also receive behind-the-scenes updates, previews, and deals for *Riyati*. If you're more of a Discord fan, join Riyati's Official Discord server — on top of a great community and instant Riyati updates, subscribers get access to Riyati's Archive Library, a *Riyati* hub for bonus short-stories, alternative PoV chapters, and character art!

Newsletter: https://riyati.ink/newsletter

Official Riyati Discord: https://riyati.ink/discord

**Long before Kylie Rae ran into the forest that fateful day, there lived another woman — Kisate Riyati, crowned princess to the Royal Kingdom of Riyati. This is her story, of how kingdoms fall and dreams are dashed.**

Just before Kisate's twenty-second birthday, she received word that the man she'd secretly loved for many years was now arranged to be her eventual husband, Takite Tanoti. Yet this news sets in motion a series of events that would not just be life changing, but ultimately instigates the destruction of the kingdom she was to rule. What was meant as a kindness to Asuza Nuueti, her primary servant and a man that long since had unrequited feelings toward her, will both save her and damn her.

Explore the beginnings of the Riyati universe, back when the Ancient Kingdom of Riyati still thrived — and see Kisate, Takite, and Asuza as they once were, long before the events of *Riyati Rebirth*.

**Get *Riyati Origins* for free today @ <u>https://riyati.ink/</u>
<u>newsletter</u>!**

moved his eyes back to the carpet. It'd been the opposite for him: barely seen Kylie but'd socialized more than ever b'fore. This past summer had more hangouts than he'd ever had, 'specially in AC'ed buildings. Could only pretend to read in the library so much b'fore they started getting bitchy, happened basically every year.

Kylie softly chuckled as she said, "I guess not." I wished Jordan knew how much of a jackass comment that'd been. He at least had the choice, ain't effectively on permanent house arrest. "Have you picked up your schedule yet?"

"Oh, uh, right." Jordan grabbed the piece of paper he'd folded and shoved in his back pocket. Dunno why he bothered — remembered everything on it, but his eyes scanned over it like he didn't. Refused to admit hypermnesia'd meant he didn't need the sheet of paper, still on his dumbass crusade against the magic that'd benefited his life. Was gonna save his life, even. "I've got Samson for homeroom, and fourth for lunch." He didn't bother mentioning the actual classes: he barely made current grade level coursework, and she's in all honors, even's in multiple AP class this year, though hadn't told Jordan yet. Was yet another weird-ass moment of watching my past play out live as Jordan's present. Kyle prob'bly had it a bit easier since no hypermnesia, but no way she ain't experiencing it to some extent too.

"Umm..." Kylie turned around, almost falling out of her chair as she did so, catching her balance at the last second. She flipped through her planner to a loose sheet of paper. "Albertson for homeroom." Her voice softened further. "And third lunch." While it ain't the first time, it's one of the core problems for this particular year: there're no shared classes or lunch periods. "Huh? Oh, sure." Kylie's eyes moved to Jordan. "Sia wanted to know what Rota's been working on you with lately."

Jordan rolled his eyes. "Dumbass's too much of a ditz to teach a damn thing." Ain't like he's the most eager learner here. Just 'cause I didn't wanna fight his ass on every little thing, made it sound like it's on me.

I knew the sigh that came from Kylie's body was Kyle. Was too amused to have been from Kylie. "Until Mom lets up, I can't really teach you. You two need to work together here."

She knew there's not a shot in hell that'd work as motivation; basically's her saying we couldn't bitch to her when Jordan didn't know shit Kylie did.

While Jordan nodded timidly, the only one who might've believed something'd come outta this's Kylie.

Speaking of, she gained control back, a softening of her gaze as her eyes didn't meet Jordan's any longer. "I, um. Guess we'll meet up after school then?"

"Oh, it's gonna be okay for you to be out again once school starts up?"

Kylie shook her head. "I doubt it, but Mom has a few evening classes in the fall so I can walk back home at least. I can't really linger but it's better than being stuck here all day."

She's desperate, and I wished Jordan got how much so. Wished he didn't nod and casually say, "Y-yeah, sure."

Wished this year would never start.

**What happens when the past seeks vengeance, the present is lonely, and the future looks uncertain?**

While Kylie survived the kidnapping incident of June, it's left her life in shambles, constantly confined under her mother's supervision or locked in her bedroom. Worse, Kylie soon learns that while Asuza may be dead, his supporters are very much alive — including a certain familiar woman from the kidnapping who knows Kylie's at fault for Asuza's demise and wants nothing more than to repay the favor.

All Kylie can do is trust Siani, even knowing Siani allowed her to be kidnapped in the first place and that Siani openly hides yet more secrets — dark secrets that could threaten Kylie's own existence. But if she can't count on her own future-self, who can Kylie trust? She'll have to decide who her allies are — and fast — if she wants to survive in this new life or else she won't make it to the end of the year.

**Buy *Riyati Rivals* @ <u>https://riyati.ink/rivals</u>!**